Millennium Stone

MILLENNIUM STONE

—◆○◆—

JACOB EMBREY

iUniverse®

MILLENNIUM STONE

This is a work of fiction. All of the characters, names, incidents,
organizations, and dialogue in this novel are either the products
of the author's imagination or are used fictitiously.

iUniverse books may be ordered through booksellers or by contacting:

iUniverse
1663 Liberty Drive
Bloomington, IN 47403
www.iuniverse.com
1-800-Authors (1-800-288-4677)

Because of the dynamic nature of the Internet, any web addresses or
links contained in this book may have changed since publication and
may no longer be valid. The views expressed in this work are solely those
of the author and do not necessarily reflect the views of the publisher,
and the publisher hereby disclaims any responsibility for them.

Any people depicted in stock imagery provided by Thinkstock are models,
and such images are being used for illustrative purposes only.
Certain stock imagery © Thinkstock.

ISBN: 978-1-4917-6125-0 (sc)
ISBN: 978-1-4917-6127-4 (hc)
ISBN: 978-1-4917-6126-7 (e)

Library of Congress Control Number: 2015903409

Print information available on the last page.

iUniverse rev. date: 04/22/2015

Spartacus Thanks You!

A percentage of each book will go to supporting the
Green Dog Rescue Project.
Visit themillenniumstone.com and greendogproject.org

Contents

ONE

THE COMING OF THE DARKNESS

William Locke's feet squashed the damp grass as he raced through a lush green field as quickly as his legs could carry him. His right arm pumped with the movement of his legs while his left arm secured a large brown ball. On his heels, four other children were in hot pursuit. But William could not look back, even when the splashing of their boots through a shallow puddle told him that they were right behind him. He was almost there. With everything he had left, he pushed his legs faster.

"I've got you!" yelled Louis, a kid three years older than Will, as he reached for Will's arm.

Thinking quickly, Will cut to the right, but this maneuver just stalled Louis for a second and allowed his friends to gain ground. William had to turn left again if he was going to make it to the goal line, but if he did, Louis would easily grab him. Then, amazingly, William's best friend, Spartacus, arrived. He was a four-legged running machine, a shepherd and Labrador mix. Louis was right on William now, his arm stretched out, and just as he was taking hold of Will's shirt, Will threw the ball to the goal line. Immediately, everyone forgot about Will and sprinted toward the ball, but they were no match for Spartacus. He pounced on the ball in no time,

1

snatched it in his mouth, and took it into the goal. He had scored the final point; William's team had won!

"We win!" William hollered as loudly as he could while bending over, gasping for air.

The other kids on William's team ran over to Spartacus and began running their hands through his short brown-and-black coat.

"Good job, Spartacus," Bismarck said, patting the excited dog on the head.

"That doesn't count!" Louis yelled. "Spartacus wasn't on your team."

"He's William's dog, so that means he's on William's team," Dante declared just as Spartacus slipped from under his hands, raced over to William, and began licking his face.

"Yeah," William said, covered in dog slobber.

"Dogs can't be on a team," another boy from Louis's team called out.

"It's not fair!" Louis yelled, and he kicked the ball with a grunt. It sailed high into the air, where the wind picked it up and tossed it into a large, dark oak. The ball bounced off a huge, towering, twisted branch and then got stuck in a fork high off the ground.

"Louis!" everyone shouted at once.

"Why did you do that?" Bismarck asked angrily.

"Spartacus doesn't count." Louis continued to whine, but he couldn't look anyone in the eye. He knew it was going to be almost impossible to get the ball.

"Now what are we going to do?" Isaac asked, looking up at the towering oak.

"Louis should have to go get it," Susan announced, and the group all started cautiously toward the giant, looming tree.

"I can't get it," Louis objected, looking timidly up into the branches. "It's too high."

"Well, it's your fault the ball's up there," Bismarck pointed out sharply.

They all stopped a short distance from the towering, twisted oak. The huge tree was long dead and hollowed out. Its bark had turned black with rot, but its limbs still bent and curved high above the grass. It reminded William of a giant dead spider, the way its branches curled inward.

Looking up at the tree in awe, the group continued to argue about who should get the ball. Will, however, was quiet, calculating in his mind the best way to climb the tree. All along the trunk were footholds where the bark had rotted away, and he was sure that once he got into the branches, he would be strong enough to pull himself up the fork to where the ball was stuck. "I can do it," he finally announced, and the group all stopped arguing and looked at him, including Spartacus.

"Will, you don't have to go up there," Susan said. "We can just get a rock and knock it down."

"That will take too long," Will countered, and he started toward the tree, but Bismarck stopped him.

"It's not the climb that's the problem," he said, looking at the tree nervously. "It's the bats that live in the trunk."

Will looked at the tree and smiled. It was true that there was a dark, ominous hole in the trunk that probably hid a dozen stub-nosed blood bats, but they didn't realize that Will had a secret weapon: Spartacus. Will called, and his short-haired brown-and-black Lab darted to him and spun around with his tail wagging furiously. "Get the bats!" Will yelled, and Spartacus darted off toward the tree for about three quick steps and then whipped around, excited but obviously a little confused. "The bats, Spartacus," Will repeated, pointing at the tree. "Get the bats!"

Again, Spartacus was off, but this time he sprinted all the way down to the tree, barking the whole way. When he reached the trunk, Spartacus stood up on his hind legs, fearlessly growling and barking into the large, dark opening, which echoed his aggression back at him. Then, suddenly, from the black orifice, a flurry of bats shot out, scattered up into the tree, and darted off. Unsure if he was finished, Spartacus looked back over his shoulder at Will, who ran to him and petted him furiously on his back and neck. "Good boy, Spartacus!" Now Will was ready to get the ball. He grabbed a handful of bark and was about to pull himself up, when he saw something that had caught the attention of his friends as well.

Slowly, he released his grip and joined his friends in common curiosity. Everyone huddled together and looked on as a parade of armor and swords marched hopelessly by. It was a troop of knights, many of whom had their helmets off, revealing expressions of despair. One knight in particular caught William's attention. He had the most elaborate armor, with a giant eagle etched on the front of his chest plate, and a huge sword with a gold handle strapped to his back. However, it wasn't his armor or sword that really caught William's attention—it was his posture. William had always thought of knights as proud, confident warriors, but this knight, in all his apparel, looked utterly defeated. His arms hung lifelessly at his sides, and his head hung low, his face draped by his long, dark hair, which was as damp as the morning around him. His armor whined with each step, and as the troops drew closer, William could begin to see dents and scratches in their armor. These knights were coming from a battle—a battle they had lost.

Some of the warriors looked at them with sadness in their eyes as they passed. The closer they got, the more defeated they looked. Then, horrifically, a knight fell to his knees and crawled frantically to William on all fours through the damp grass. As soon as he reached him, the knight grabbed William's shirt and began to sob.

"I'm so sorry, boy!" he cried. "I'm so sorry we couldn't stop it. I should have died out there. I'm so sorry!"

William didn't know how to react, so he just stood there and let the man cling to his shirt until one of the other knights pulled him to his feet and carried him off back into the line of beaten men. Too frightened to do anything, the children just watched as the knights passed. Once the last one had disappeared into the distant fog, the kids finally started to look at one another again.

"Where do you think they came from?" Marie asked, finally taking a moment to wipe some dirt from her face.

"Who knows?" a short boy answered.

"Hopefully far away," Louis said, still looking at the spot in the fog where the knights had disappeared.

Spartacus began to whine, so William placed a hand on his head to calm him, which seemed to help both of them. Petting Spartacus was something that could always cheer both of them up.

"Well, do you want to play another game?" Bismarck asked the group, returning his gaze to the branches of the twisted oak, where the ball was still lodged.

The group seemed to snap out of a trance as they all looked back at the tree.

"We haven't finished with the first game," Louis countered.

"Oh, don't start that again." Bismarck spat. "You guys lost fair and square, and besides, we can't even play another game until we get the ball."

William turned around and was just about start back toward the tree, when a distant shout caught his attention. It sounded a lot like his name.

"William! William!"

It was his name, and this time everyone else heard it too, because they all turned toward it. In the distance, running as fast as she could, little Elizabeth was closing in quickly.

Spartacus immediately saw this as a game, so he tore off after her and nearly knocked her to the ground when he jumped on her.

"William! Come fast," she called out, now fighting off Spartacus's slobbery tongue. "Your father needs you, and the king is at your cottage!"

"What!" everyone, including William, yelled at once.

"King Herodotus is at your home! Right now!" Louis shrieked.

William's eyes nearly popped out of his head. "Why is the king at my cottage?"

"I don't know!" Elizabeth yelled. "Go find out!"

By now, all the other children were staring at William, trying to figure out what was so special about him. William, on the other hand, still had not moved. He had never been around a king and wasn't sure he was supposed to be around one while covered in mud.

"What are you waiting for?" Louis finally called out. "The king is waiting for you!"

Even this didn't register with William. It wasn't until Spartacus jumped up and licked his face that he snapped back to reality. Dirty or not, the king wanted to see him. So he darted off. A couple of his friends fell in behind him, and the group wound its way through the village streets. After a couple of left turns and then a right past the large village inn, he suddenly stopped in his tracks, and his friends almost ran into him. In front of his humble home was the royal carriage, pulled by four huge Clydesdale horses. The carriage itself was painted deep red, and gold tassels hung from every edge. The horses, which towered over William, were covered in red silk caparisons, which were also lined with gold tassels.

"Wow!" Bismarck said. "The king's carriage!"

William just stood there, petrified. He had seen the king's

carriage before but only from a distance—and never sitting in front of his home.

"What are you waiting for?" Dante said, and he nudged Will forward.

Cautiously, William made his way around the carriage and to his own door, where another surprise waited: two of the king's guards. They were covered from head to toe in shining gold armor, with flowing bloodred capes that stopped just above their ankles. They each held a long silver spear as tall as they were; the blades, twice the size of William's head, gleamed ominously in the sun.

At first, William didn't dare move. He just stood there at the bottom of the steps to his home, staring helplessly up at the golden guards. Spartacus, however, was unimpressed and sauntered right through the guards and into the house. The two guards took little notice of the dog, so William decided to give it a try, and, to his amazement, neither of the guards so much as looked at him as he ventured into his cottage.

"Spartacus" was the first thing he heard his dad, John, say. "William, where are you? Come into the common room, Son—don't be afraid."

With his dad's encouragement, William found the courage to step into the common room. There in the middle of the room was King Herodotus. He was not a tall man, about the same height as William's dad, but he was dressed much more lavishly. He was covered in silk garments and a thick red robe lined in white fur, topped by a shiny gold crown encrusted with red and white diamonds. Other than his attire, he looked like any other person William had ever seen. He had a nose, a mouth, two blue eyes, and dark-brown hair. To the king's right was a man dressed in stark contrast. He was a bit taller than the king and dressed in a single blue gown covered in silver stars, with a tall blue hat. He had a long white beard; long, flowing white hair to match it; and bright green eyes that followed William as he walked cautiously into the common room and stepped beside his father and Spartacus.

"So this is William," the king said with a comforting smile.

Suddenly, William felt an elbow in his shoulder, and he looked up and noticed that his father was nudging him. "Bow, William."

"Oh, it's quite all right," the king said, still smiling. "I'm the one who should be paying my respects to him."

The last comment caused both John and William to cast the king confused looks, at which the king began to laugh. However, his laughter quickly died away and was replaced by a somber expression.

"Are either of you familiar with the Millennium Stone?" the king asked.

Father and son looked at each other. William had no idea what it was, and by the look on his father's face, neither did he.

"No, Your Majesty," John finally said.

"Well, a thousand years ago, the people of this great kingdom began to lose hope."

"In what, sire?" John asked before he realized that he was interrupting. "Sorry."

"Ask whatever you wish. You, of all people, have a right to know," the king continued. "No one knows exactly, but suddenly, people started to fall into despair. All around the kingdom, for a thousand miles in every direction, people were falling into depression." The king started to pace as he went on. "It was said that life became a chore and was no longer enjoyed. Food became bland; people stopped using sugar and spices. Birthdays were no longer celebrated, and children"—the king paused and looked down at William—"stopped playing in the streets. The kingdom was truly in a state of sadness." The king's eyes drifted to William's father.

"But what was born from this hopelessness was something of the greatest evil. It was a creature of shadow and smoke, and it began to devour the land and all the people in it. Armies were sent against it, but they too were swept aside and devoured. This thing, this creature, was unstoppable—until out of nowhere, a man showed up with a crystal-blue rock that was burning in white flames."

"The Milleneanium Stone?" William said.

"The Millennium Stone," the king said, correcting him with a grin. "That's correct. It's a powerful stone with a magic that nobody understands, not even my friend Voltaire," the king said, gesturing to the man in the blue robes and the long white beard, "and he is a great wizard."

Voltaire smiled humbly.

"With this stone, the stranger was able to defeat the great Darkness single-handedly. And when the Darkness was defeated, all the land rejoiced, and happiness found this kingdom once more. So the Millennium Stone was taken to a monastery at the top of Mount Inkedu; there it was put under the protection of a society of monks who vowed to protect it. And it was there that the stranger who brought the stone revealed a secret to the monks that would forever keep the Darkness away. But they"—the king paused and looked deep into William's eyes—"have forgotten it, and now the Darkness has returned."

William's father stumbled back and almost tripped over a small wooden table. "What does that mean, and why have you come to us?" John asked frantically after regaining his balance.

King Herodotus calmly looked over at his friend Voltaire.

"The monks on Mount Inkedu have failed—every one of them," Voltaire said calmly. Then he added cheerfully, "But there is hope."

At that statement, Spartacus decided to add some of his own thoughts with a loud bark. Voltaire smiled at the dog and then reached out with his long fingers and scratched him lightly behind his left ear.

"And that hope is you, young William," Voltaire said, looking at him.

William had no idea what to do or say. He didn't know about this Darkness and was pretty sure he didn't want to know.

"How is my son involved in this?" John asked.

"I had a vision," Voltaire said, "of William fighting the Darkness."

"Alone?" John asked.

"Yes," Voltaire answered.

"That's preposterous!" John began to rant. "He's just a boy, barely twelve years old! He's not going to fight that thing, Your Majesty; that's what you have armies for."

"I have sent my armies, John," the king replied evenly.

"And they were beaten," William said. "I saw them in the field where my friends and I were playing."

"That's correct," said King Herodotus.

"Then what chance does my boy have?"

"Please, Mr. Locke," Voltaire said politely, "allow me to continue."

John took a deep breath and put his arm around William.

"There is a prophecy that has surrounded the Millennium Stone for as long as we have known about its existence," Voltaire continued. "Simply put, it says that there is a boy who knows the secret of the stone, and he must go to it alone and whisper the secret into the Millennium Stone to revive its power and defeat the Darkness."

"Did you say 'alone'?" John asked.

"I did," Voltaire answered.

"But I don't know any secret!" William said. He had no idea what this secret was. How could he? He hadn't even known about the stone's existence until five minutes ago!

"You may not now," Voltaire said in his calm voice, "but you will once you see the stone."

"This is absurd, Your Majesty," John said. "I'm sorry, but I will not allow my son to venture off alone to Mount Inkedu."

"I know this is hard for you to accept, John," said Voltaire, "but your son is our only hope."

"How do you know that your vision was right?" John asked, tears beginning to swell in his eyes.

"I am certain."

John still did not fold; he stood there looking into the desperate eyes of his king and shook his head. "My son is not going anywhere."

William was pleased to hear his father say that. He had no idea where Mount Inkedu was, and he wasn't convinced that he was the right boy. He was just the son of a blacksmith; surely, the boy meant to do this task was the son of a great knight. However, deep inside, William was invigorated by the thought of venturing out into the wilderness. He sometimes fancied himself a great explorer who would discover new forests and lakes and maybe even meet a dragon. *On second thought, maybe this adventure is for me.*

"John, will you and your son take a ride with me?" the king asked after a moment's hesitation.

With a calculating look, John agreed with a nod. Then the five of them, including Spartacus, climbed into the king's carriage and took a long ride through town. William and Spartacus both kept their heads hanging out the entire time. Spartacus did it just for fun, but William, on the other hand, stuck his head out so that if anyone who knew him walked by, he or she would be sure to see him in the king's carriage. After they made their way through town, they started up a large hill that flanked the west side of the town. It was a steep climb, but the Clydesdales didn't seem to struggle. Finally, they reached the top of the hill, and the coach came to a halt. Spartacus leaped out as soon as the door opened, followed by everyone else.

The view of the town was striking. Hundreds of little houses surrounded the king's castle, which was an edifice of gray stone that towered above the many buildings around it. William could see people running through the streets like ants, and small puffs of smoke rose out of the occasional chimney.

"Where's our house at, Dad?" William asked, trying to find it within the maze of roads and cottages.

"I don't know if we can see it from here, Will," John answered. "I think it's on the other side of the castle."

"As beautiful as this view is, John, it's not what I wanted you to see," said King Herodotus. "Please follow me."

The group followed the king to the west side of the hill, and there on the distant horizon was the Darkness. It looked like a storm cloud of ash and night. From this distance, it looked as though it weren't moving, but its sheer size was intimidating. William couldn't imagine what an army of knights could have possibly done against it. Fighting it would be like fighting a tornado.

"It just looks like a black cloud," John said, staring at it.

"A black cloud that can take any form," Voltaire said, "and will do so with the most malevolent intentions."

"It is coming, John, and it is going to destroy everything," the king said solemnly. Then, in a show of compassion, he reached out and took Mr. Locke's shoulder. "If William stays, he will be killed like the rest of us, but if he leaves, he may have a chance to save us all."

William heard these words, as did his father, and looking out into the great despair stalking them all, William thought about his friends and family, who were busy playing and working in the town below. Then he thought about Spartacus and all the other dogs, cats, and birds that were dashing through alleys, running through fields, or enjoying the warmth of a fire, and he decided that he was going to save them. He was going to save everyone.

"I will go," William said, and the tall wizard smiled at him.

John, on the other hand, took a deep breath and then swallowed hard. William could tell that his father was trying not to cry, but it was okay if he did, because he was scared too. His dad had once told him that bravery was not the lack of fear; rather, bravery was the continuing on in the presence of fear—so he would be brave.

Spartacus nuzzled William's hand and then crawled close to his side.

"I will allow him to go," John finally said, staring at his son, "but with one condition."

"Yes?" King Herodotus said patiently.

"He must be allowed to take Spartacus."

Hearing that, the wizard let out a mighty laugh and then announced in a thunderous tone, as if to the whole town, "And so it shall be—the hero, William, and his dog, Spartacus. We surely have nothing to fear!"

The optimistic power of that statement sent a shimmer of hope through all their hearts, as well as Spartacus's tail, which began wagging furiously. William was ready for his journey.

TWO

THE SHADOW IMP

F ar away, the Darkness approached, and deep within its malevolent heart echoed the name William Locke. This evil spirit possessed a wicked intelligence that knew instantly that a warrior had been dispatched to destroy it. But it was prepared. The Darkness had at its disposal three powerful assassins who, when summoned, would seek out and destroy the would-be slayer. The first of these assassins was the Shadow Imp; he was a cunning creature with the ability to affect those with weak minds—those who acted on every impulse without a thought of the consequences. However, this creature of shadow and ash existed outside of human perception and could only be seen in short glimmers at the periphery, which were almost always shrugged off as nothing. So the Darkness went to work, and soon the Shadow Imp emerged. It was no bigger than a child's foot, was as black as night, and had glowing red eyes and translucent wings that beat as quickly as a hummingbird's. Then, in a flash, it was off and seeking William Locke.

◄o►

William spent the rest of the morning with his father, the king, the wizard, and, of course, Spartacus. He packed a small sack with some food for himself and Spartacus, as well as a blanket for the nighttime, and then he joined the others for an early lunch.

Just as William was finishing his last bit of stew, King Herodotus returned from a quick trip out to his carriage. He held a rolled-up piece of parchment, which he flattened out on the table.

"Come here, my young champion," the king said, beckoning William over. "This was a map of my entire kingdom, but what you see here is just your journey."

William looked down and saw a piece of parchment that had been torn on the left and right sides, leaving a long middle piece.

"You are here," the king said, pointing to the castle drawn at the bottom of the map, "and you must get here." The king moved his finger up the length of the paper, to a mountain at the top. "You must make haste, William, because time is of the essence. However, do not be foolish in your journey; go around the Crystal Canyon, as it's far too dangerous to go through. You will also want to stop at Potemkin Village for supplies and a good meal. Then continue north around the Witchwick Marshes. Again, do not risk a trip through, because there are witches there who will jump at the chance to eat a boy your age." The king paused for a moment to let the thought sink in, which it did. William swallowed hard at the thought of being eaten by witches. "From there, continue on to Mount Inkedu in Mountain Shadow Forest. The temple is at the summit of that mountain."

William couldn't believe the journey he was about to embark on, but he drew strength from knowing that Spartacus would be with him. With a nod, King Herodotus rolled up the map and gave it to William, who stuffed it into his bag.

"Well," the king said encouragingly, "it's time for you to go, brave William. But I have one more thing for you." King Herodotus reached into his robe and pulled out a small leather bag. "It's a bit of gold that I want you to take. Buy whatever you wish with it. It is to aid you on your journey."

"And what about a weapon, Your Majesty?" Will's father asked.

"I'm afraid not," Voltaire answered. "He has taken all that he can."

His father had a concerned look as Will slung his bag over his shoulder and headed to the door. Then William found himself in his dad's embrace.

"Be careful, William," John Locke said, doing his best to choke down his emotions. "You're a strong boy, but only fight when you have to. If you can run, then run."

"I will, Dad," William said as he returned his father's hug with everything he had. Then they both let go and headed out the door.

From his own house to the edge of town, Will was escorted by a regiment of the king's best guards, King Herodotus, Voltaire, and his father. As he walked through town, out of the corner of his eye, he could see his friends looking on in amazement. He wanted to call out to them and tell them what he was about to do but decided he shouldn't; this was not a time to brag. Once they reached the town's end, he gave his father another hug, and then he was off with only Spartacus at his side. Behind him, the whole town watched. William didn't think many of them knew what they were looking at: just a boy and his dog venturing north.

"Well, Spartacus, it looks like it's just us now. I hope we don't let everybody down."

Spartacus replied with an encouraging bark, and it was exactly what William needed to hear. It seemed that the farther they got from town, the more nervous he became—because the journey became more real. William sometimes dreamed about being a great explorer, so he knew how to tell direction by the movements of the sun, but he had never been so far outside of town that when he turned around, it was gone. He was now just about to reach that point, so with a short pause, he turned and took in a last look at the distant castle.

"This is it, Spartacus; a few more steps and there will be no turning back."

Spartacus let out a soft bark that, to William, sounded like a question, so William answered it. "Because people are counting on us, including Dad." Spartacus barked again, this time with more oomph, and William gave him a pat on the head before he turned and continued on.

Rolling hills of golden wheat stretched for miles in front of them. The tall stalks came up to William's waist, which meant they were just over Spartacus's head, causing him to leap through the stalks like a furry frog. His black-and-brown coat glistened in the high sun.

"Let's see," William said out loud. "What could the monks ask me that I know the answer to that nobody else does?" William folded his brow as he began to think. "I know how to shoe a horse. I know how to forge a sword. I know—hey, look at that." Stretched out in front of William was a small dirt road scarred with the gashes of wagon wheels and hoof prints. It was headed roughly north, so Will decided they could follow it; that way, Spartacus wouldn't have to keep jumping. So on they went as Will continued to rack his brain, trying to figure out what he knew that was so special.

Unfortunately, after an hour of winding through the tall grass on the small dirt road, Will had not thought of anything he considered special knowledge, so he decided to give up for the time being. Just as he did, he heard the unmistakable sound of horse hooves clopping behind him. A bit startled, Will glanced over his shoulder, and sure enough, there was a convoy of horses in the distance. Many of the horses were pulling wagons filled with goods that were covered by dirty white sheets. Mixed in with the horses was a group of men scattered alongside each of the wagons.

"Look, Spartacus—traders," Will said, and Spartacus's tail began to wag slightly. Will had always had a small affinity for traders because they got to travel from town to town, buying and selling all kinds of neat things, from fruits to saddles and even weapons. In fact, whenever traders came to Will's town, he and his friends were always the first to arrive and see what exotic things they were selling. Even now, Will was tempted to ask them if he could see their goods. But as his thumb stroked the small bag of gold at his side, he decided it would be better if he didn't. He knew he might need the gold for something important later, though he had no idea what it might be.

As the convoy started to get closer, Will could faintly hear their conversation over the clopping of hooves, and to his surprise, they were talking about him.

"You think that boy's lost?" a deep voice asked.

"He must be," another answered. "All the way out here without his parents."

Will continued to walk while listening as closely as he could without looking as if he were listening.

"Maybe he's out hunting," another voice said.

"Along a trader's road?" the first voice answered incredulously. "I don't think so. He's gotta be lost."

Will suddenly realized that he had slowed down considerably while trying to listen to what they were saying, which had allowed them to get much closer. Will thought they couldn't be more than thirty feet behind him now, but he still refused to turn around. Spartacus, on the other hand, was not so shy. He dropped back behind Will and began barking playfully at the coming group.

"Hey, boy!" one of the men called out in a high tone, obviously talking to the dog. "What are you doing out here?"

Spartacus suddenly darted back over to Will with his tail flailing; it was obvious that he wanted to meet these new strangers. William stepped into the grass and waited, hoping they would just pass by. If they didn't, he would have to figure out something to tell them. It was not as if they would believe him if he told the truth anyway—a lone boy off to save the entire kingdom? To be honest, he didn't know if he believed it himself yet.

As the first wagon began to pass Will and Spartacus, the latter of whom was now waiting impatiently by his side, a tall man in brown trousers and a dusty white shirt looked down curiously at Will.

"Hello, boy," the man said, and Will recognized his voice immediately as the deep one he had heard from the start. "What are you doing out here all alone?"

"I'm going to Potemkin Village to see my uncle," Will said, quickly making up a story, and then he started walking alongside the inquisitive stranger to be polite.

"Potemkin Village—that's quite a distance from here," the same man continued. "Where are your parents?"

"They're at home—sick," Will said hesitantly. He'd never been good at lying and didn't like doing it, but there was no way they would believe the truth. To save time, he figured this story would be easier.

"Hmmm," the tall man answered. "Well, that's where we're going too, so if you want, you and your friend can tag along with us."

That idea didn't sound bad to Will. He knew that he was supposed to be alone, but his journey around the Crystal Canyon was going to take him a few days anyway; it might be neat to travel with a bunch of traders. Besides, even though Will had just met them, they didn't seem as if they would be the kind of people who would want the Darkness to destroy everything.

"Sure," said Will. "You know, I've thought about being a trader myself one day."

"Is that right? Well, I'm Frederick Douglass, and behind me is Rutherford Hayes." Rutherford, another tall man, gave a polite nod as William looked back at him. "Over there is Aaron Burr." William could barely see him from behind the horses, so Aaron raised a hand to let Will know that he was there. "And I'll introduce you to those guys in the back once we make camp. And you are?"

"My name's William, and this is Spartacus," he said, patting the dog on the head.

"Spartacus, huh," Rutherford said. "Is he friendly?"

"Oh yeah," Will answered. "He wouldn't bite anybody."

"Yeah, he looks like a friendly pup," Frederick said, and then he bent down and scratched Spartacus behind the ear. "Well, we've got a long way to go yet, so if you get tired of walking, William, we can put you up on one of the horses."

"Oh, I'll be fine. I'm used to being on my feet all day. My dad's a blacksmith."

"Is that right?" Frederick said as his eyebrows hit the top of his head. "Does that mean you know a thing or two yourself?"

"Oh yeah, I help my dad all the time," William said, feeling proud of himself. *Maybe I will make a sword that will defeat the Darkness,* he suddenly thought to himself.

"Well, we have a few old, dull swords that could use a sharpening," Frederick said. "If you could do that for us, we will pay you for it."

"Sure," Will said. He'd sharpened plenty of swords for his father before.

"All right then," Frederick said cheerfully. "You see, guys? We've needed those swords sharpened for ages now, and then along comes William—that's what I call good luck."

Hearing that, William had to smile; it was good to feel needed. So the group continued on while Frederick and the other traders shared stories of their travels. William couldn't help but get excited about the tales of elves and witches, and he wondered if he would have any stories after his journey. But one thing was for sure: Frederick wasn't kidding about them having a long way left to go. They ventured through the rolling fields of wheat and into a sparsely populated maple forest. The leaves were beginning to turn orange for the coming fall, which was magnified by the low sun showering gold rays through the canopy above. Then, just as the sun touched the horizon, they came to an open meadow. Frederick gave the order to circle the wagons, and Will stepped aside while the traders brought the wagons into a ring. The horses were unstrapped from the wagons and brought inside the circle so that they could graze and rest during the night. Everyone else unrolled a blanket and began to settle in while Aaron started a fire.

Like an earthbound northern star, the fire lit by the traders acted as a directional beacon to the Shadow Imp. The moment the fire was lit, the Shadow Imp saw it. Soon, it thought, it would find William and fulfill its duty by destroying him.

Will and all the traders except Frederick, who was rummaging around under the sheet of his own wagon, gathered around Aaron's fire, which was now heating a pot of soup large enough for everyone. Spartacus, who seemed to be as tired as Will, was curled up next to him by the fire.

"Will, have you met everybody yet?" Rutherford asked after testing the soup with a large wooden spoon.

"No, not yet," Will answered.

"Well, sitting across from you are George, John, Thomas,

and James," Rutherford said, pointing to each one as he went. When he was finished, they all raised a hand and said hello at once.

William waved back, but by the time that short greeting was done, he had already forgotten half their names. Before he could say anything, Rutherford announced that the soup was done, and everyone was on his feet, dipping his bowl into the pot, including William. The soup was hot and thick and full of potatoes and ham. William couldn't have asked for anything more. He ate half the bowl himself and then placed it on the ground for Spartacus, who went to work immediately and finished it off.

"Here they are," Frederick announced as he pulled four swords from under the sheet of his wagon. Then he walked over and placed them noisily next to Will. "These are the swords that I was talking about. What do you think—can you sharpen them?"

Will picked up one of the dullest ones and inspected it as Frederick scooped some soup for himself and took a seat.

"Yeah, it shouldn't be too hard."

"Great," Frederick responded between bites. "Sharpen all four of them, and I'll give you three silver pieces. Sound fair?"

A day ago, three silver pieces would have been a fortune, but since the king had given him the small pouch filled with gold, which he still had strapped to his side, suddenly, three silver pieces didn't seem like much. But he was still grateful for the offer. "Sure, that sounds great," he said.

Meanwhile, weaving its way through the maple trees like a black hummingbird, the Shadow Imp finally arrived at a ring of wagons with a fire in the middle. Quickly, it darted through the grass and then up into the air and landed on one of the horses, which gave out a wild neigh that everyone ignored. From its perch, the Shadow Imp could see everyone, including William, and knew that it was time to begin. But first, it had to discover which of these men were weak minded and easily controlled, starting, of course, with William himself.

Leaping from the horse, it shot toward William.

"So, William," Aaron said, "mind if we call you Will?"

"No," he answered.

"Will, then, you're from Castle Village, right?"

"Yep," Will said.

"How do you like living right next to the castle?" George asked.

"I grew up there my whole life, so I don't really know what it's like to live anywhere else, but it's nice, I guess."

This answer made some of the men laugh for some reason. Then, in the middle of their laughter, William suddenly felt a need to find out what it would be like to step into the fire. In fact, more than anything, he wanted to know what it would be like to jump right in the middle of the fire. For a second, he almost got up to jump in, but just before he did, he reasoned that jumping into the fire would burn him horribly, and he had no desire to find out what that was like. So he shook off the thought and returned his mind to the conversation at hand.

William's mind was stronger than the Shadow Imp had hoped, but no matter—at least some of the men around him were bound to be weak minded. So it moved on.

"Have you ever seen the king?" Thomas asked.

"Sometimes," Will answered, careful not to say too much, "when he goes out hunting or something like that."

"Have you ever talked to him?" James said.

Again, William found himself feeling that he had to lie, so he answered quickly and then decided to change the subject. "No. But I have a question."

"Shoot," Frederick said, stroking a sleeping Spartacus.

"Why do we have to go around Crystal Canyon? Wouldn't it be faster just to go through it?"

"You don't know about Crystal Canyon?" John asked. Then, for no reason, he took his bowl of soup and poured it over his own head. As soon as he did it, he leaped to his feet, screaming about how hot it was. The rest of the group stared at him in amazement.

"John! What in the king's name did you do that for?" George hollered.

"I don't know," John said, frantically removing his shirt and using the dry end to clean off his head. "I didn't even realize that I was doing it."

The others in the group exchanged odd looks before returning their attention to Will.

"Anyway," Rutherford continued, "the reason we don't go through Crystal Canyon is because there's a dragon that lives somewhere deep inside."

"A dragon!" William replied excitedly as a smile crept across his face.

"Yeah, a big one, too," James added. "A hundred feet long with a two-hundred-foot wingspan."

"It's not that big," George countered. "I've seen it."

"You've seen it!" Will gasped.

"Yeah, a couple of us have," George continued. "It feeds on the deer in this forest."

"So how big is it?" Will asked, gaping.

But George didn't answer. He was too busy watching James remove his trousers and throw them into the fire. Then, as soon as his pants hit the flames, he snapped out of whatever trance he had been in and frantically tried to rescue them. But it was too late; they were already consumed by the flames.

"What the heck did you do that for?" George said.

"I don't know," James said, dumbfounded. "I just thought ... I don't know."

"What in the world is going on?" John spat, and he and James shared confused looks.

Then Rutherford began to sing. "I'm a little teapot, short and stout. Here is my handle; here is my spout." As he sang, he created a handle with his left arm and a spout with his right. "When I get all steamed up, hear me shout; tip me over, and pour me out." With that final verse, he leaned over to the right and said, "Shhhhhhh."

Suddenly finished, Rutherford froze, still tilted to the side, and began looking at the confused faces staring back at him. Slowly, everyone started to come to his feet. Will thought that this was odd behavior but that maybe they were just playing a joke, so he alone stayed seated next to Spartacus, who had become alert all of a sudden.

"There might be a witch nearby," Aaron whispered intensely as he began scanning the forest around them.

"I've heard no incantations," John said, still alert.

"She might be whispering," Aaron answered.

As the group waited in silence with only the crackling of the fire, William noticed Thomas begin to make his way to the swords by his side. Nonchalantly, he bent down and picked up one of the longest blades. This action brought Will to his feet, and subtly, he began to back away.

"What are you doing with that sword, Thomas?" Frederick asked as everyone's attention shifted to the weapon.

But Thomas didn't answer. It became clear that he was in the same trance the other men had experienced. Without thinking, Frederick lunged at his friend and tackled him to the ground. Amazingly, that didn't snap Thomas out of it. It was clear that he still had something to do, and he wouldn't stop until he had done it. William backed up quickly. He wanted to help but didn't know what to do, so he started to call Spartacus to him. However, he noticed Spartacus's head darting to and fro. He was watching something—something William couldn't see.

Meanwhile, Aaron joined Frederick in restraining Thomas.

"Thomas, let go of the sword!" Frederick yelled, but Thomas would not let go. Instead, he started to fight even harder.

William decided he should join them. He wanted to offer whatever help he could. Then, out of the corner of his eye, he noticed Rutherford pick up a sword, and at that moment, Spartacus was focused on Rutherford's shoulder. That was when it hit him: William suddenly realized that Spartacus could see what was making everyone act so strangely, so he yelled out, "Get it, Spartacus!"

In a flash, Spartacus was off. He was jetting back and forth and all around the campsite. Darting back toward William, he leaped into the air and slammed into James, who was nearly knocked off his feet. Obviously missing his target, Spartacus landed awkwardly, but as soon as his feet were back under him, he was off again, sprinting toward John, who instantly started running the other way.

William's attention fell back on Rutherford, who was approaching him with the dull sword. Just as William started to back up, he felt someone grab him. James had clutched both of his arms and was holding William in place as Rutherford approached. Then Rutherford lowered the point of the sword to William's stomach and reared back as if he were about to thrust, when George tackled him into the dirt.

"What's the matter with you, Rutherford?" George screamed as he pinned him to the ground. But just like Thomas, Rutherford was not stopping. While it was apparent that he didn't want to hurt George, he was fighting with all his might to get back to his feet and over to Will.

"Let me go!" William shouted, but James didn't release him, so Will began stomping as hard as he could on James's right foot. However, James did not so much as flinch. Then, as Spartacus whizzed by James again, James began to carry Will to the fire.

Frederick and Aaron were still struggling with Thomas, and George was wrestling with Rutherford. William knew there was one more guy, but he couldn't see him, and he was almost at the fire. Thinking fast, he kicked the pot hanging above the flames, which still had enough soup in it to extinguish the fire. This small act seemed to confuse James; with no more fire to put Will in, he suddenly paused and released his grip. William leaped away as soon as he could and then instinctively checked on Spartacus, who was still chasing an invisible target. Now, however, there was someone chasing Spartacus—John was racing after him. Fortunately, he was no match for Spartacus's speed; however, he was unrelenting. As Spartacus zipped under wagons and around horses, John followed without regard for his own safety. A horse kick narrowly missed his head.

As for Frederick, he was finally able to wrench the sword from Thomas's hands, but this just gave Thomas two hands to wrestle with, allowing him to overpower Aaron and send him tumbling back into a wagon. Aaron's head hit hard on a wheel, knocking him out cold. In a flash, Thomas sprang back to his feet and dashed for another sword. Soon Thomas and James both had swords and were closing in on William.

Frantically, Frederick threw down his sword, and he was about to tackle both of them when George came out of nowhere, seized Frederick by the waist, and hurled him to the ground. Just then, Rutherford joined Thomas and James with swords. William had nowhere to go. He was surrounded by men with swords. Then, horribly, he heard Spartacus yelp. John had his leg.

After seeing that the dog was captured, the Shadow Imp stopped just behind the three swordsmen and hissed, "Kill him." The three men raised their swords; as they did, John let out a scream. Spartacus had bitten him and pulled free. Before the Shadow Imp could dash off, it saw the jaws of a dog close around its body.

With his arms raised protectively, William saw Spartacus land squarely behind the men advancing on him, his jaws clinched. Then Spartacus began shaking something violently, his head snapping back and forth. Suddenly Thomas, Rutherford, and James dropped their swords and looked at one another as though they had all just shared the same nightmare. John and George soon joined them.

Frederick climbed to his feet and made his way to Aaron, who was just coming around.

"Are you all right, Aaron?" Frederick asked.

Before answering, Aaron took a look around, and when he saw the confusion on everyone's faces and realized that nobody was trying to kill anybody, he answered, "I'm fine. Just have a bit of a headache."

"I'm sorry, Will," Rutherford said, taking a knee in front of him. "I don't know what came over me."

"No," Will said with his eyes to the ground. "It's my

fault." *It is time to come clean.* The king and wizard had told him that he had to travel alone, but he hadn't listened to them. He had almost gotten himself and Spartacus killed because of it. "I'm on a quest to beat the Darkness that's going to destroy everything," Will confessed. He expected a series of incredulous scoffs, but none came. On the contrary, the traders were all looking at him in silence, waiting for more. "I have to travel north to a temple, and that's where I'm headed, just me and Spartacus. I would have told you sooner, but I didn't think you would believe me."

At that, Frederick laughed and then said, "We probably wouldn't have, but I think we all do now."

"That's for sure," James said. "But why did we try to kill you?"

"I think there was something controlling you," William said. "Something we couldn't see, but Spartacus could."

"An imp," Aaron said. "I've heard of them and of their power over people."

"Well, more may be on their way—so, Will, it would probably be best if you left now, for all our sakes," Frederick said sorrowfully.

"I'm sorry all this happened," Will said as he called Spartacus with a pat on his leg.

"Don't apologize," Aaron said, finally bringing himself to his feet.

"Is there anything you need for your journey?" Thomas asked. "We'll give you a discount."

"Thomas," Rutherford scolded.

"I'm just kidding," Thomas said, trying to lighten the mood. "But really, do you need anything?"

"I don't think so," Will answered. "I think I have everything."

After a moment of silence, the group gathered around Will, and each took a moment to pat him on the back and wish him good luck. John even took a moment to apologize to Spartacus, who was quick to forgive. Then William and Frederick made their way out of the camp until they were a good distance from the wagons.

"Will," Frederick said, pulling something from his boot, "I want you to have this." In his hand was a small but visibly well-crafted dagger. It had an amber handle with a four-inch blade that was safely secure in a leather sheath. "I picked this up a couple of years back, and it has served me well. Hopefully you will never have to use it, but here you go."

William accepted it gratefully. "Thank you."

"You're welcome. Now, north is that way," Frederick said, pointing behind him. "If you keep walking straight, you'll walk right into the Crystal Canyon. From there, you can either walk around it—but you'll probably run into more traders—or you can go through it. If you decide to do that, keep your head down, and move fast; chances are that you won't run into the dragon."

"Thanks again," Will said with as much of a smile as he could muster.

"Don't mention it. Now, good luck, and next time I'm in Castle Village, I'll try to find you."

With that, Will was off. Once again, it was just him and Spartacus.

THREE

The Crystal Dragon

Spartacus and William marched on into the night until they came to a cliff that William almost didn't see. The moon was cloaked in the sky by a dense cover of clouds, so there was almost no light to navigate by, and if it hadn't been for Spartacus's echoing bark, William might have stepped right off the edge.

"Well, I think this is a good place to stop, Spartacus," Will said as he dropped his bag and then tossed his blanket out over a patch of damp grass. "Come on, boy."

With that, Will lay back on his makeshift bed with Spartacus curled up next to him. But his mind couldn't relax; he kept thinking about the imp, if that's what it was. From what he remembered in school, imps could only affect the weak minded, or people who were quick to follow orders. So if William was going to have any company, they would have to be strong minded. But how would he know who was strong minded and who wasn't? It looked as if he were going to have to remain alone with Spartacus through the whole journey. Looking down at his loyal friend, William decided that was not a bad thing. Spartacus had already saved his life once, and they just had started. Hopefully he would get a chance to return the favor.

31

After that last thought, William drifted off to sleep, and to his amazement, he slept well under the stars. In the morning, he was pulled into consciousness by a wet tongue that kept licking his face. Wiping the slobber from his cheeks, he sat up and took a moment to enjoy the warm sun shining down on him. Then, slowly, he opened his eyes to the most beautiful sight he had ever seen. Stretched out before him was Crystal Canyon, gleaming with a rainbow of sparkling color. Reds, blues, greens, purples, and many other brilliant colors shone radiantly as far as Will could see to his right and left. The low eastern sun was aligned perfectly with the canyon, igniting the entire expanse in a spectrum of colors. However, to Will's surprise, the canyon was not wide; it looked as if it were no more than a mile across.

"What do you think, Spartacus?" William asked as he pulled a length of salted beef from his bag, broke it in half, and gave one of the pieces to Spartacus. "Should we go straight through? We could probably get to the other side before noon."

Will waited for some kind of reply, as he often got one when talking to Spartacus, but Spartacus was too busy gobbling down his strip of beef to talk. So Will continued.

"We don't have a lot of time, and I really don't want to run into any more traders. So you know what, Spartacus? Dragon or no dragon, we're going through the Crystal Canyon!"

With that, Will stuffed the rest of his stick of beef into his mouth, stood up, and began scooting the blanket from under Spartacus. Instead of moving, Spartacus just lay there gnawing on his strip of beef while Will pulled and tugged. "Spartacus," Will said, "move." Spartacus looked up innocently at his friend but still didn't budge. In a final heave, Will yanked the blanket from under his friend and, with a frustrated scowl, stuffed it into his bag. "Thanks for your help," Will added, and Spartacus's tail started to wag.

Cautiously, Will stepped to the edge of the canyon and looked straight down. The jagged crystal wall dropped abruptly for hundreds of feet. There was no way they were going to climb down there. "Come on, Spartacus—we have to find a place where we can climb down," Will said, and they started off along the ledge. For half an hour, they traveled and found nothing suitable for their descent. Just when Will was about to give up, Spartacus barked—he had found a shallow ledge that dropped slowly into the canyon.

The crystals were sharp and jagged; Will was going to have to be careful on his way down. He grabbed the edge to steady himself as he took his first steps into the canyon, and he could feel the sharp crystals jabbing into his palms. Worse, Will could tell that the terrain wasn't any easier on Spartacus's paws. As they traveled farther down, Spartacus often tested a couple of spots before putting his weight on any particular leg. Just in case, Will made it a habit to check on him every few steps to make sure he was okay.

About halfway down, Will started to regret going through the canyon. His palms were raw, and Spartacus was beginning to whimper. Will couldn't imagine how his paws were feeling. Then, suddenly, Will heard the high-pitched sound of breaking crystals screeching toward him, and when he looked up, he saw Spartacus sliding out of control straight for him! He dug his hands into the crystals and leaned forward. He was going to have to stop Spartacus as well as keep himself from being knocked off the ledge and into a landscape of jagged crystals. With a thud, Spartacus slammed into his chest, and Will gripped the rocks as tightly as he could. The sharp crystals punctured the palms of his hands, but if he let go, he and Spartacus would tumble off the ledge, so he held on with all his might.

Spartacus struggled frantically to get his feet under him, but he was trapped at an awkward angle and began squirming desperately. In the commotion, Will's grip started to falter; he was going to have to do something, or they were both going to fall. In an awkward turn, he shifted his body sideways and lifted his knee so that Spartacus could use it as a balancing point, which he quickly did. With only a single slip, Spartacus managed to find his balance just before Will's grip failed him. With the pressure off, Will peeled his hands off the jagged ledge. Tiny trickles of blood dribbled down his palms, but luckily, none of the wounds were deep, so he wiped his hands on his pants and turned to make sure Spartacus was okay.

"Be careful, boy," Will said, stroking him with the back of his hand so as to not get any blood on his coat. Spartacus turned compassionately and began licking Will's face. "Okay, okay. You're welcome."

The climb became easier the closer they got to the bottom. The ledge descended more slowly, and there were no more abrupt drops that Spartacus had to leap down. It was a smooth walk as long as they stayed close to the canyon wall.

As they made their way down, a vexing aroma began to emanate from the canyon floor. The closer they got to the bottom, the stronger the smell became, until Will's nostrils felt as if they were on fire. However, as strange as the smell was, Will felt as if he knew it from somewhere. Then, as he looked down at his companion and saw Spartacus try to shake the smell from his snout, it hit him: the smell was ammonia. The whole canyon reeked of ammonia. Without thinking, Will pulled his shirt up over his nose, which helped a bit, but it was something that Spartacus couldn't do. Thinking fast, he began rifling through his bag until he found an extra shirt, which he tied precariously around Spartacus's snout. At first, Spartacus wasn't sure if he liked it and tried to paw it off his face. But after taking a few filtered breaths through the shirt cloth, he seemed to quickly decide that it was worth the trouble. Side by side, they ventured on, noses covered.

Will took his first step from the canyon wall onto a soft layer of crystal sand. His first thought was that this part of the journey was going to be much easier on Spartacus, and with a light crunching under their feet, they continued along the canyon floor. Will would have been able to enjoy the scenery more if it hadn't been for the smell, but the canyon was undeniably beautiful. There wasn't a single spot that wasn't covered by crystals. Everywhere he looked, he saw greens and purples, blues and reds. Some crystals were as small as needles, while other crystals were larger than Will himself. However, as beautiful as everything was, Will couldn't forget about the dragon. Any chance he got, he scanned the sky above him or looked cautiously into a crystal cave. Fortunately, he didn't see anything. On the other hand, not knowing where the dragon was seemed just as bad as seeing the dragon; if he could see the dragon, then at least he wouldn't feel as if he were being stalked.

Then something in the distance caught his attention. It was movement of some kind, and William froze stiff with Spartacus just behind him. With a wave of his hand, Will told Spartacus to stay as he ventured slowly forward. Around a small bend of huge red crystals, Will found the source of the movement; it was a lake. It stretched out farther than Will could see and was dotted with crystal islands. For a second, the lake looked inviting, especially since Will didn't have any water to drink. But as he approached the transparent liquid, it became clear that the odor burning their nostrils was coming from the lake. It was a giant lake of ammonia-saturated water.

"Spartacus!" Will called out in a loud whisper. "Come on. This place is pretty, but I can understand why the traders don't go through it. It just poi—"

Will couldn't have finished that last word if he had wanted to, because it was then that he noticed one of the islands move. Focusing as hard as he could, Will suddenly froze. The island was not an island at all—it was the crystal dragon! The name was perfect. The creature was made of as many dazzling crystals as the canyon itself. Every scale was a radiantly colored crystal of blue, green, red, or purple, and as the creature moved, each one glistened in turn. Will was hoping with all his heart that the dragon had not seen him or Spartacus. It seemed to have its back to them, but it was turning and stretching as though it had just awakened from a nap. At one point, it stretched its head in one direction and its tail in the other, showing its entire length to Will. While it wasn't as big as the traders had made it out to be, it was much larger than Will.

Spartacus seemed to immediately understand the danger they were in, and he was the first to start to back away. It was then that Will realized he was on the shore of the lake with nothing around him to hide behind. Swiftly but quietly, he began to back up. The dragon stretched its head into the lake and began drinking generously, gulping down swallow after swallow of ammonia-filled water. With the dragon distracted, Will saw this as his moment to run, but as he turned, his foot caught a crystal. He stumbled noisily, almost falling backward into the lake. Frantically, William spun around to see if the dragon had heard him, and it had. Its fierce crystal-armored face was pointing directly at William, and in one swift movement, the dragon leaped into the air with a powerful beat of its wings, glided effortlessly across the lake, and then slammed into the shoreline in front of Will. Its tail hit the lake like a giant paddle, splashing water high into the air.

Petrified, with Spartacus cowering behind his legs, William could only stare into the stormy blue-green eyes of the crystal dragon.

"Who are you?" the crystal dragon roared in a voice

that sounded like a thousand crystal wine glasses singing in perfect harmony.

The power of the dragon's voice made Will step back, but he ended up stumbling over Spartacus and barely managed to stay on his feet.

"I'm William," he said meekly, unable to take his eyes from the dragon's fiery gaze.

"Why are you here?"

"We just needed to get to the other side of the canyon."

"We?" the dragon said skeptically.

"Me and Spartacus," William said, but when the dragon did not respond, he clarified. "My dog."

The dragon tilted its large head, and a shimmer of color moved across its face. For a moment, it looked at Spartacus, which made him shrink even farther behind William. Then the dragon drew back to its full height, towering over William.

"Unfortunately for both of you, you have decided to trespass when I am hungry," the dragon said, looking down on both of them.

"Does that mean you're going to eat us?" Will asked, hoping desperately that the answer was no.

"No. I will only eat one of you," the crystal dragon responded smoothly. "You must choose who it will be— yourself or the creature cowering behind you."

"I don't want you to eat either of us," Will said a little more frantically than he would have liked.

"You should have thought of that before you contaminated my home with your presence," the dragon said with a harmony almost an octave higher.

"Well, I'm sorry," Will shouted back. He was still scared for himself, but he wasn't going to let anything hurt Spartacus, no matter how big it was. "But I have to get to Mount Inkedu as fast as I can, or the Darkness is going to destroy everything."

This fact seemed to catch the dragon's attention, and its expression changed from threatening to curious.

"I have seen this Darkness," the dragon said pensively, and then it lowered its head to William's level. "You are the one who is going to save us?"

"Yes, but I can't do it without Spartacus."

"The dog?" the dragon confirmed skeptically.

"Yes," William answered, feeling a bit more confident.

For a long moment, the crystal dragon stared at William. He felt as if its eyes were penetrating his soul. Then, all of a sudden, the dragon brought himself back to his full height and glared down at William and his dog.

"No," the dragon said in piercing harmony. "I will eat one of you. So choose which one it will be."

"You will not touch Spartacus!" William yelled. Spartacus had already saved Will's life once, and he had made the promise to do the same, even if it meant being eaten by a dragon.

"Then your choice is made," the dragon roared. It reared up and lunged forward. Its mouth was wide open, with jagged crystal teeth coming right for William's body, but Will did not move. He would not run and leave Spartacus to be eaten. However, just before the dragon's jaws surrounded William, Spartacus sprang forward, snarling and barking with a fury that William had never seen. The dragon stopped and drew back, looking on, amused at this tiny creature so fiercely protecting his friend. Then, amazingly, the dragon seemed to smile. All the rage had left its eyes, and slowly, it lowered its head back to William's level.

"You are both very brave and quite noble." The dragon's voice was now much lower but still in beautiful harmony. "Perhaps this kingdom has a chance after all, with you as our hero and your friend as a guardian."

Will didn't know what had just happened, but relief was

beginning to wash over him. It seemed that Spartacus was feeling relieved as well, as he had backed up and was now standing calmly beside Will.

"But I am a creature that believes in fate, and I do not think you came to me by accident," the dragon said as it broke a small crystal from its body and held it out for Will to take. "If at any time you should need my help, all you must do is break this crystal, and I will know where you are as though it were a spot on my own body, and I will come to your aid." Will took the crystal as the dragon continued. "But do not use it unwisely, because I only offer it once."

Will nodded. It took him a few breaths before he could say, "Thank you."

"Now," the dragon said, back to its original harmonic tone, "go on. You have no time to lose. May you have good fortune on the rest your journey."

With that, the dragon's wings unfurled, and with a great leap, it exploded into the air. With its tail swaying behind it, the crystal dragon flew off and vanished behind a wall of crystals.

William was awestruck. Dumbfounded, he gazed at the small red crystal in his hand. It was barely the size of his pinkie, but it had the power to summon a dragon. Carefully, he placed it in his pocket; then he knelt down and took a moment to praise Spartacus.

"I don't know where I would be without you, Spartacus," Will said, scratching him in his favorite place, right behind his left ear. Then he picked up the shirt that Spartacus had removed during his frenzy and secured it again to his friend's nose. Now unafraid, the two of them made their way out of the Crystal Canyon. In fact, the ascent was much easier with the weight of their fear of the dragon off their shoulders.

FOUR

POTEMKIN VILLAGE

William's eyes opened slowly and sluggishly in the early morning light. In the distance, he could just make out the broken line of rooftops that was Potemkin Village. He and Spartacus had arrived at this spot late last night, and Will had decided it would be better to enter the town in the morning rather than at night. Even though he'd desperately wanted to find an inn, he'd figured that after what had happened with the traders, it would be best to avoid people at night altogether. He had slept soundly and now felt refreshed except for an ache in his shoulder, which was no doubt an effect from sleeping on the hard ground. After a long stretch and a quick massage, Will packed away his blanket and pulled out two strips of beef and a bread roll that had been baked hot and fast, which had made it hard. Then the two of them started into town.

The beef didn't last long with either of them. Spartacus managed to gobble his down in a few bites, and Will was right behind him. The bread roll, on the other hand, was another matter. It was as hard as a rock, and the best Will could do was gnaw at the corners, chipping away at it a piece at a time. Ten minutes later, Will had managed to finish half of it, and it wasn't a tasty half at that. Eating it was like chewing on chalk, so he tossed the rest of it to Spartacus, who leaped on it instantly.

"You can have the rest of that," William said as he watched his friend devour it with his strong jaws. "I think it was made for you anyway."

The roll was gone in no time, and soon William and Spartacus had wandered onto a wide dirt road. As they followed it toward Potemkin, it continued to get more crowded until they reached the gates to the village, where a constant stream of people were coming and going. Travelers of all kinds were around him. Some were dressed lavishly in silk robes, but most of them were dressed like William, in simple shirts and trousers. Spartacus was getting excited by all the people, and his tail was wagging furiously as his head darted from one new thing to another. William wanted to calm him down, but he was feeling similarly, and as he entered the main gate, he was sure that if he'd had a tail, it would have been wagging as much as Spartacus's was.

William was surrounded by shops. The main road into town was a huge and colorful bazaar. Of course, being from Castle Village, he was familiar with large markets, but there was something different about this one. It was more exotic. In Castle Village, all of the stores were owned, so it was the same old people selling the same old stuff every day. But here, William could see traders who had just come into town setting up shops along the road. It seemed that anybody who wanted to could set up a shop, and because of that, anything and everything that one could possibly have wanted was there. A great rush of excitement hit Will when he remembered he had a pouch of gold at his side. *Look out, market—here I come.*

With so many sights, it was hard for William to concentrate on any one shop, but then the heavenly smell of flame-kissed turkey hit his nostrils. Off to his left, a vendor was using a huge fan, waved by a tiny dwarf, to blow the smoke of his barbecue into the crowd. Will could not resist, and neither could Spartacus. They darted over, and William made his first purchase: a giant turkey leg, which he generously split with Spartacus. After that, they wove their way through the street, looking at all the wonderful things available for him to buy. There were stores with colorful scarves and booths with amazing jewelry that reminded him of the Crystal Canyon. Seeing these made him pat his pocket where he kept the fiery-red crystal that the dragon had given him. Also accompanying the sights were the voices of the vendors as they yelled out at every passerby.

"The finest scarves made entirely of elfin silk!" one man hollered as he held a pair of deep-blue scarves high up so that they gleamed in the sun for all to see.

"The finest jewels in the kingdom; come take a look!" another man yelled.

"Come all," declared another man, who was dressed similar to Voltaire, the king's wizard, in a blue robe with stars; his stars, however, were gold, and they were beginning to peel off the dirty blue fabric. "I will tell you your fortune. For a mere piece of silver, I can tell you the day you will die!"

William hurried past him; he had no desire to know when he was going to die, whether or not the man was honest. As he continued on, more voices shouted at him from either side, and more colorful sights flashed by. But above the commotion, a new voice began to thunder. It was louder than the vendors' voices and carried with it a greater authority. Will, like many others, followed the voice to a tall man with long white hair and a thick white robe to match. He was standing on a small wooden stage and hollering into the crowd.

"People of Potemkin," he shouted, "do not take me as a fool or an eccentric prophet; I speak the truth! And if you do not heed my words, it will most certainly mean the death of you!"

William found himself as enticed as everyone else and was soon wading into the crowd of people who surrounded the charismatic speaker.

"A great Darkness is coming, and it is going to destroy everything in this fallen kingdom! The wicked deeds of our king have created it, and you all"—he continued swinging his finger from one side of the crowd to the other—"will be the ones to suffer because of him."

William didn't like what he was hearing. The king was the one who had sent him. He was trying to save everyone.

"You can try to pack and flee on your own, but the Darkness will find you, and you will suffer more for it."

"But what is the Darkness?" a man in the front cried out.

"It is the hatred and malevolence that can only be spawned within the cavity of a king with an empty soul," the man in the white robe said. "And it will soon be here to destroy this town and everyone in it!" His last words roared as though he were trying to tell the whole village. "However, there is hope."

For a second, Will thought the man was going to mention him, so he tried to make himself as small as possible.

"If you donate to me by dropping whatever gold you can into this wood box," he said, pointing to a large pine box tilted slightly so that as the coins were dropped through a small slit, they would hit wood and then roll noiselessly to the rest of the coins below, "then perhaps we can survive. With this gold, I plan to buy whatever rations I can, and I will lead you all to the safety of the Engordii caves."

"But you said there was nowhere to hide," another voice called out, this time from a middle-aged woman.

"For you, yes, but I know of a place that, through my incantations, can protect everyone who hides there. We will need to stay there for many weeks, perhaps even months. But when the time comes and the Darkness has passed, we will be able to emerge, ready to start a new kingdom with a just king who will not allow such wickedness to pass!"

With this last statement, Will decided that he had heard enough, and before he could stop himself, he was yelling out, "If the king is the reason for the Darkness, then why is Castle Village still standing?"

The crowd's attention shifted to Will, and he instantly wished he hadn't said anything.

For a long second, the tall, white-haired man's dark eyes glared at Will. "The king created the Darkness far from his own castle, so as to avoid blame," the man said, and then he shouted louder than ever. "But as it destroys his kingdom, the king does nothing!"

"He has sent an army against it!" William replied angrily.

"And it has failed!" the man snarled. "Hope is lost."

"Hope is not lost!" William said, and the man on stage glared at him once again. "The king—" William started, but just as he did, he felt someone grab his arm and begin leading him away from the stage. When Will looked up, he saw an unshaven man with long black hair and a sheriff's star on his dirty brown coat. He led Will forcefully away from the crowd and then released his arm with a shove. Spartacus snarled angrily at the large man but didn't attack.

"You're done causing trouble, boy," the sheriff said, and then he started to walk away.

"I'm not causing trouble," Will countered. "That man doesn't know what he's talking about. He's just scaring everyone."

"Archduke Aquinas is saving everyone, if you had bothered to listen," the sheriff hissed over his shoulder. "Now, if you come near him again, I will throw you in the stocks."

A bit shocked at what he had just been told, Will watched the sheriff disappear back into the crowd of people. "I guess they'll find out soon enough—won't they, Spartacus?" Will said, scratching his friend behind the ear. "Well, come on—let's buy some things and get out of here."

Spartacus seemed to agree, as he gave an energetic bark, and the two of them started down the street again. However, Will didn't get two steps before he heard a vendor who seemed to be talking to him directly.

"You there, boy," the vendor said, and Will started cautiously toward her. She was an old woman whose face was covered in a thin red scarf wrapped hastily around her head and neck. Tanned, wrinkled skin surrounded her bright blue eyes and continued down her long, bare arms. She was also possibly tall, but her crippled posture and hunched back brought her down to Will's height. In front of her was a series of stacked crates, each displaying some kind of colorful elixir. "Come, boy," she continued, trying to draw him closer with a bony finger.

Will and Spartacus stepped cautiously forward and stopped just in front of her precariously constructed stand. Clumsily, she reached down without taking her eyes off William and began fumbling for something that was apparently just out of her reach. Continuing to struggle for it, she forced herself to bend a bit lower. "Got it," she announced softly, and her hand emerged with a vial of clear liquid. "You will need this for your journey, boy," the old woman said as she placed it on her stand.

Will slowly reached for it, but he was slapped on the hand with surprising zeal by the old lady.

"Do not touch!" she snapped. "Not until you buy it."

Will withdrew his hand and gave Spartacus an awkward look, which the dog returned with a tilted head and a small whine. "What is it?" Will finally asked.

"It is an elixir with a most mysterious power." The old lady's voiced crackled slightly. "You must use it when the time is right."

"And when will that be?" Will said, a bit impatient with all the riddles that seemed to be surrounding his life at the moment.

"How should I know?" the old woman retorted. "You're the one on the quest."

"How do you know that I'm on a quest?" Will asked skeptically.

"I know many things," she replied. "You are on a quest for someone very important, the mission for which many people are counting on you."

She is vague but accurate, Will thought.

"And you don't even know what this does?" Will asked again while bringing his nose close to the vial.

The old lady mimicked his movement so that she was face-to-face with him across the stand, the vial of clear liquid between them. "I have no clue, but it must do something amazing considering how expensive it is."

Will quickly brought himself to his full height. "How much is it?"

"Three quarters of the amount of gold that you have on you," she said.

"What! It's not worth it," William spat.

"Oh, I assure you it is," the old woman said confidently.

Will looked down at Spartacus, who raised his ears and eyebrows in the same motion. Then he heard the woman speak again, but this time, her voice contained a seriousness that Will could not ignore.

"Do not overthink this. Decisions like this must be made from your heart, not your mind."

Will looked once again at the clear vial and couldn't help but feel that perhaps he should buy it. It would cost him nearly everything, but where he was going, gold probably wasn't going to help him. On the other hand, a potion might save his life.

"Fine, I'll take it," Will said, and he reached for his money pouch—but it was gone! Searching frantically, he couldn't find it anywhere, and then, suddenly, he noticed that Spartacus was gone too. Will spun around and caught sight of his dog's tail just before it disappeared into the crowd. An instant later, William sprinted after him, and as he did, he heard the old lady say as loudly as she could, "I'll save it for you."

Zigzagging through the crowd, Will soon caught sight of Spartacus weaving his way between people in a clumsy swiftness that knocked a lavishly dressed man right off his feet. Face first, the man plunged to the dusty dirt road, cursing the whole way. Will jumped over him so that he wouldn't have to break stride and then pushed even faster. He saw Spartacus dart around a corner, and Will followed. Thankfully, as soon as he made the turn, he saw that Spartacus had stopped, but he was not alone. He was barking at a girl with dirty-blonde hair, bright blue eyes, and a bit of a frightened look on her face.

William finally stopped at Spartacus's side, panting heavily. "Did you ... take ... my gold?" he asked in breaths.

The girl looked at Will, raised his small leather pouch, and then said, "Oh, is this yours?"

"You know it's mine," Will shot back.

"No, I don't," the girl replied calmly. "I found it on the ground."

"You did not! It was hanging on my belt."

"No. It was on the ground."

Will hesitated for a second but then quickly decided that he would have heard that much gold hit the ground. And even if he hadn't, Spartacus would have noticed for sure, just as he had caught her picking it from his belt.

"No," Will said at last. "Admit it; you stole it, and Spartacus caught you. And if you don't give it back, I'll tell him to bite you."

"Is Spartacus your name?" the girl asked, bringing all her attention to Will's dog, and in an instant, his tail began to wag. "You're such a cute dog. Come here, boy." With that, Spartacus jumped to her side and then sat there in ecstasy as she immediately found his favorite spot just behind his left ear. "You wouldn't bite me, would you?"

Will was dumbfounded. He couldn't believe that Spartacus was being so friendly. "Spartacus, come here," Will commanded, and Spartacus quickly returned to his side with his head low.

"Aww. Don't yell at him," she scolded.

"I didn't yell," Will replied defensively, but he did feel a little bad for scolding him. He never liked disciplining Spartacus, even in those rare times when he deserved it.

"Well, poor Spartacus—he just knows a good person when he sees one," the girl said.

"Then give me back my gold."

"Fine, if money is all you care about, then here," the girl said, and she tossed him the leather pouch, which Will caught in midair.

With the money back in his hand, Will began to question whether or not he might have dropped it, and he decided maybe he shouldn't be so hard on her. But just as he was about to say something, a familiar voice came at him from the crowd; it was the sheriff.

"Well, well, well, what do we have here?" the sheriff said as he marched closer. "Looks like the pickpocket's been hard at work."

By the look on the girl's face, she had dealt with this sheriff plenty of times before. "I didn't steal anything; I found it," she said belligerently.

"Yeah right, girl," the sheriff spat. "Looks to me like you need another day in the stocks."

Will quickly decided that he didn't like the sheriff either

and would rather help out the girl, who, apparently, was Spartacus's new friend. "She did find it," Will said. Then he added while looking at her, "And she gave it back to me."

"Gave what back?" the sheriff asked.

"My gold," Will replied, and he held up his small pouch.

The sheriff quickly snatched it out of his hand and began to weigh it in his palm. "There's at least twelve gold pieces in here. This isn't yours," the sheriff said loudly, and then he dropped the bag into his own coat pocket. "I think I just caught two thieves today."

"What!" Will yelled, and Spartacus began to growl. "That's mine! You can't—"

"Quiet, boy!" the sheriff ordered. "I can do whatever I want—I'm the sheriff." Then he grabbed Will and the girl in one motion and began dragging them into the crowd. But he didn't get far; Spartacus darted around him and began snarling and snapping at the sheriff.

"Get him, Spartacus!" the girl yelled, and Spartacus lunged, but the sheriff kicked wildly with one of his large brown leather boots and managed to strike Spartacus across the jaw. With a howl, Spartacus stumbled back.

"Hey!" Will screamed, and he began to fight however he could, kicking and struggling against the sheriff. Suddenly, he remembered the dagger that Frederick had given him, but foolishly, he had stuffed it in his bag that morning, and there was no way he was going to be able to get to it. So he began hitting the sheriff with the bag itself, but it was doing little good, and if anything, it was just frustrating the sheriff more.

"The more you fight, the longer you stay in the stocks," the sheriff scolded as he dragged them away once again, ignoring William's protests. Spartacus was still growling but was now keeping his distance.

As the sheriff pulled them through the streets, people

were quick to step aside and even gave Spartacus a wide berth. Unfortunately for Will and his companion, the stocks were not far away and were just outside the sheriff's office.

"Cortez!" the sheriff yelled, and a lanky man with black hair and a big nose came stumbling out of the sheriff's office in a clumsy hurry. "Open the stocks!"

Cortez fumbled through a ring of keys and then opened two stocks that were side by side.

"Lock her up," the sheriff commanded as he shoved the girl toward him. After a surprisingly brief struggle, the girl acquiesced and placed her hands and neck into the stock to be locked in. Will, on the other hand, tried to yank himself free, but the sheriff's grip was too strong. Almost effortlessly, he ripped William's belongings away from him and then secured his hands and neck in the stock. In no time, William and the girl were both trapped, bent over with their hands and heads stuck in two wooden posts.

"Find a rope, and tie that mutt to one of the other stocks," the sheriff said, scowling at Spartacus. "And if he bites you, kill him."

"Don't you dare touch my dog!" William screamed.

"But you don't let these troublemakers go until I say so. And no food or water either!" the sheriff shouted, ignoring Will's protests, and then he tossed his bag into the office.

"Yes, sir," Cortez said with a nod; then he glared at a snarling Spartacus.

The sheriff turned to his prisoners. "If you two keep your mouths shut, maybe I'll let you out tomorrow morning. So stay quiet!"

William had never been so angry in his life, and as much as he wanted to shout and scream at the sheriff as he walked away, he managed to restrain himself. He knew that wouldn't help his situation; it would be best to let the sheriff leave. Then maybe Cortez would help him.

51

"Mr. Cortez," William called out as he stepped back out of the sheriff's office, this time with a rope. "You have to let me out. I can't be stuck here."

"You be quiet," Cortez snapped. "You heard what the sheriff said, so keep your mouth shut!"

"Sir," William pled, "the sheriff stole my money, and I need it back."

"Shush, boy!" Cortez said, and then he turned his attention toward Spartacus and started slowly approaching him with a noose. "Come here, doggie," he squeaked, but Spartacus was ready. He was crouched low with his lips curled high, showing an intimidating set of pointed white teeth. Cortez hesitated, and Spartacus lunged a couple of inches forward and barked with a ferocity that sent Cortez sprinting frantically back into the sheriff's office, crying out, "Bad doggie," as he ran.

William would have laughed if he hadn't been in the predicament that he was in, but right now, he needed to find a way out. For a second, he thought about the crystal in his pocket that the dragon had given him, but there was no way he could break it in his present situation. And even if he could, he didn't think he wanted to. He wanted to save the crystal for a life-or-death situation. While it would have been fun to see the look on the sheriff's face as the crystal dragon freed him and took back his gold, he was certain that this was not the time to use the gift. Curious to see what the girl was doing, William turned his head awkwardly to his left and noticed her wiggling her hand back and forth. With each motion, her hand disappeared farther and farther into the hole until a final slip, and it was free.

"These stocks are old, and they can't hold small hands like mine," the girl said as she wiggled her fingers under the stock for Will to see.

"But how will you get your head out?" Will asked because

there was no way she was going to be able to wiggle her head out through the small neckhole.

"With these," the girl said, and she held up a key ring she had pulled from her pocket.

Will recognized the keys immediately as the ones Cortez had used to lock them up in the first place.

"You are a pickpocket," Will said a little louder than he meant to, and then he added, "And you did steal my gold."

"Yeah, and I'm sorry. But I'm trying to get us out of this, so can you tell your dog to watch Cortez?"

William was taken aback by her nonchalant attitude, but she had a point—they needed to get out before Cortez discovered what was happening. "Spartacus, guard the door, boy," Will said, gesturing futilely with his hands, and Spartacus darted forward, barking at the door.

In no time, the girl had unlatched her own lock and was free. Then she swiftly opened Will's stocks—and none too soon, as Cortez was at the door once again, this time with a bow and arrow. Clumsily, he started to pull back the string, but before he could aim it, Spartacus leaped at him, clamped down on the soft wood, and then stripped the weapon easily from his hands. Again, Cortez found himself running scared back into the office.

This time, Will and his new friend shared a laugh, and when they were done, Will turned to her and asked, "What's your name?"

"Liliu Okalani," she said, still smiling.

"Well, Liliu," Will said, "my name is Will. Thanks for letting me out, but I need my gold back; there's something that I have to buy. And since you're the reason I got it taken in the first place, you have to help me get it back."

Liliu gave him a long, calculating look and then said, "I'll tell you what. I'll help you get it back, but it will cost you three gold pieces."

"What! You're the reason I'm in this mess, remember?"

"I gave your gold back to you, remember?" Liliu said smugly. "That creepy sheriff is the real thief."

William couldn't argue with that. She might have stolen it in the first place, but she had given it back—something the sheriff was definitely not going to do. "Fine, but I'm only giving you one gold piece."

"Two it is," Liliu declared, as though they had come to an agreement. "But I'm going to need a distraction, not to mention we're gonna have to make sure that Cortez here doesn't go anywhere."

Will thought for a moment, figuring he wasn't going to bother arguing about the two pieces of gold, and then a plan came to him. "I know the perfect distraction."

Liliu smiled slyly, and the two of them turned toward the sheriff's office.

"But first," Liliu said, "let's give Cortez here a taste of his own medicine."

With that, Will and Liliu opened the door to the sheriff's office, and Will yelled in, "Cortez, come out with your hands up, or I'll send Spartacus in to drag you out." Not two seconds later, Cortez came walking out with his hands high. Under the watchful eye of Spartacus, Liliu locked Cortez in the stocks while Will ran into the office and grabbed his belongings. Then the three of them headed toward a large crowd of people surrounding a booming voice.

"All right," Liliu said, "you get the sheriff's attention so that I can get your gold back, and then once I'm at a safe distance, I'll make sure that he sees me. He'll start chasing me; I'll lose him."

"You're sure you can lose him?" Will said.

"I've done it before. He just caught me off guard this morning," Liliu answered confidently. "Then I'll meet you at the potions stand in five minutes."

"You promise you'll be there?"

"I promise. Now, how are you going to get his attention?"

"Just watch," Will said, and he was off. Keeping an eye out for the sheriff, he navigated through the crowd of people until he came to the stage where the man in the white robe was roaring. After a deep breath, Will stepped onto the platform.

At first, Archduke Aquinas didn't notice Will's presence, as he was lost in his speech. "Your small donations of gold can save your lives as well as those of many others. Tomorrow we leave and escape the reign of a wicked king who brought this undeserving nightmare upon us. Donate now and—"

"The king is not wicked," Will interrupted as loudly as he could without screaming, and he was surprised at how quickly everyone's attention fell on him.

"You again," Aquinas hissed under his breath.

"This man doesn't know anything," Will hollered, immediately noticing the sheriff at the back of the crowd, slowly start to move toward him. "He's only trying to scare you so that you'll give him gold."

"Lies!" the archduke screamed. "Is the Darkness coming? Yes, it is! Has the king been able to stop it? No, he has not! He has given up himself and has fled his own kingdom, leaving us to suffer!"

"No, he hasn't!" Will screamed back. He was starting to get angry. This man with the white robe and white hair was lying to everyone. He was a thief, just like the sheriff, and William was not going to let him get away with it. "I am from Castle Village, and the king is still there, and he has personally sent someone to defeat the Darkness!"

"Who?" a man cried out from the crowd. "Whom has he sent?"

"A great knight?" another asked.

"Or a powerful wizard?" somebody else said just as Will

saw Liliu sweep by the sheriff and no doubt pick the gold from his pocket.

Will hesitated. He thought about telling them that the chosen one was a knight or a powerful wizard, but then he would be no better than the liar next to him, even if the lie did sound better than the truth. "But a simple truth is better than the greatest lie," his father had once told him. So he would risk everything and tell them the truth. "No. He has sent me."

Instantly, the crowd broke into laughter, including the tall man onstage next to him.

"You!" Archduke Aquinas howled. "You! Then the king is crazier than I thought!"

The crowd burst into another bout of laughter. Will could even see the sheriff chuckling—that was, until he saw Liliu holding up Will's pouch of gold on the other side of the crowd. But when she took off running, the sheriff didn't follow; he just scowled at Will. Their plan was not going the way Will had wanted.

"Thank you," Aquinas said as he pretended to wipe away a tear. "I needed a good laugh."

"It's not a joke," Will said adamantly. As everyone started to laugh again, Will noticed that one man wasn't laughing. He was elderly and held a twisted wooden walking stick in one hand and a gold coin, outstretched and about to drop into the box, in the other. But before he let it fall into the slot, he stopped and brought it back into his pocket. Apparently, the man in the white robe noticed this.

"You, sir," Archduke Aquinas called down to him. "You would put your fate in the word of this boy?"

The old man paused for a long moment and then said in a raspy voice, "Yes."

This seemed to catch the crowd's attention, and any last giggles ceased immediately.

"Then you must be senile," Aquinas declared so that everyone in the crowd could hear him.

"Not yet," the old man reasoned, and then he turned to face his accuser. "But the way I figure it, I've been listening to people like you my whole life—always tellin' me what I should be doin' and where I should be doin' it. But this boy has said to keep on doin' what you're doin' and have faith. And I like that. Look, I don't know if you can really protect us from this Darkness; maybe you can. But I've seen a lot of dark times, and I'm tired of hiding from them. This time, I'm gonna face it, just like this boy here. And then maybe the Darkness won't come back."

Archduke Aquinas was clearly at a loss for words, and his hesitation spoke volumes. Soon those in the back started to wander off, and those in the front began to talk among themselves until one of them spoke up.

"I want my gold back."

This seemed to snap Aquinas back to the present. "You already donated it. It's too late."

"Well, hey," another man cried out, "if that money was really for us anyway, then you should give it back."

"Hold on," the archduke said, but he was soon drowned out by protests.

Then Will noticed the sheriff start forward once again. At first, Will was going to flee, but he soon realized that the sheriff wasn't heading toward him; he was going toward the gold-donation box. The white-haired man was calling him over. They were in this scheme together!

Shoving people right and left, the sheriff soon reached the box of gold and spun around, drawing his sword at the same time. "Get back!" he ordered. He began thrusting the tip of his blade into the air, forcing people to stumble back.

"Hey!" a man yelled. "That's our gold! What are you doing?"

"It is not your gold," the sheriff growled. "You gave it away!"

"They're a couple of con men!" a man in the back yelled, and the group pressed forward but stopped in front of the sheriff. No one wanted to risk getting too close and getting stabbed.

Archduke Aquinas quickly realized what was happening. As fast as he could, he jumped down beside the sheriff and began emptying the gold from the box into a large leather bag. A few brave men tried to stop him, but the sheriff jabbed at them, and they found themselves stumbling back into the crowd.

"Stay back!" the sheriff roared. "All of you!" In a scream of pain, the sheriff dropped his sword. Will immediately looked down and saw that Spartacus wasn't by his side; he had snuck under the platform and was biting the back of the sheriff's leg! In a flash, two men from the crowd darted forward and tackled the sheriff to the ground, while a heavy-set woman kicked the sword away and then began to wrestle the bag of gold away from the archduke. Soon everyone was piled on top of the sheriff or his con-man friend. In the commotion, Will managed to hurry off unnoticed.

"Spartacus, come," Will called out, and the agile dog snaked his way from under the platform and back to Will's side.

The two of them hurried down the dirt road until they returned to where this whole ordeal had started—at the potions stand. Waiting for them was Liliu. She was smiling from ear to ear with gold in hand.

"Here you go," she said. "And I already took my share."

"Thanks," Will said, and then he turned to the old vendor with the red scarf. She already had his vial out and was waiting for him. He gave her the rest of his gold, except for one final piece, and then took the potion, wrapped it carefully in a shirt, placed it in his bag, and returned his eyes to Liliu. "Well, I guess that's it. Maybe I'll see you on my way back."

Liliu was silent for a moment, but just before Will started to walk away, she asked, "Is what you said true?"

"About what?"

"About being the one who's supposed to stop the Darkness?"

Will hesitated. He knew that he had just shouted the information out to a whole crowd, but there was something about telling it to Liliu that seemed more serious. "Yes," he finally answered.

"Let me come with you."

Will was a bit surprised that she asked so bluntly, yet a part of him had been hoping she would ask, even though he knew he would have to tell her no. "I was told that no one is allowed to go with me," Will said, and his mind jumped to the memory of the traders.

"Who told you that?" Liliu asked.

"The king and a wizard."

"Oh," Liliu replied. It seemed that she knew she couldn't argue against that.

"Yeah," Will said apologetically. "But if I could, I would definitely ask you if you wanted to come."

"Really?" Liliu said as her eyebrows hit the top of her head.

"Yeah, I guess," Will replied nonchalantly, trying not to sound too eager.

"Well," Liliu began, "what if you told me where you were going, and I decided to go there too, and I just happened to be going the same way you are?"

Will thought about it for a moment, and while the king probably wouldn't have thought it was a good idea, his dad probably would have. And as good a travel partner as Spartacus had been, he wasn't good for conversation. *So why not?* Will thought, and then he vocalized his decision. "Sure, that sounds like a good idea. I'm going to Mount Inkedu, in Mountain Shadow Forest.

"What a coincidence," Liliu said, beaming. "That's exactly where I'm going."

"I'm about to leave."

"So am I," Liliu said with a smile, and the two of them started north past the stocks, which were now filled with the sheriff, Archduke Aquinas, and Cortez. Then they left the village at the north gate. But just as Will cleared the large wooden doors, he stopped and turned to Liliu.

"Don't you need to tell your parents that you're leaving?"

Liliu shrugged and said, "I don't have any."

"Oh," Will said sadly. For a second, he thought about asking what had happened, but he decided that now was not the time. So they left Potemkin Village in silence, heading north to Skyreach Forest.

FIVE

SKYREACH FOREST

Furious, the Darkness thundered at the Shadow Imp's failure. The first assassin was dead. However, the Darkness soon calmed and, in its belly, began to form the second assassin. This creature was feared by all who knew it. It had a powerful grasp that none could escape, and it reveled in crushing the life out of its foes: it was the Night Anaconda, a swift and silent assassin that would stalk one in his or her sleep and then slowly squeeze the life from the person. From the Darkness, it slithered into the light. The sun's rays were swallowed by the depth of the blackness of its scales. Like a passing void of darkness, it crept through the land on its way to find William and devour him.

As soon as they had wandered past the gates of Potemkin Village, William remembered the dagger that Frederick had given him, and he decided he would never again put it somewhere where he couldn't reach it. He opened his bag and began rifling through it. The knife had wrapped itself in his blanket, and William had to twist the dagger a few times before he could pull it free; then he tucked it securely in his belt.

"What's that?" Liliu asked after watching the commotion.

"It's a dagger that someone gave me. I wish I'd had it when that sheriff arrested us."

"Can I see it?" she asked as she held out her hand.

Will hesitated for a moment. The memory of all the men trying to kill him was still fresh in his head, and he didn't want to hand over his one line of defense to a new acquaintance. "Not yet," Will finally said a little shyly.

"Why not?" Liliu protested.

"Well"—Will hesitated again—"you wouldn't believe me if I told you."

"Try me," Liliu said with a patient expression.

"Okay," Will said. He proceeded to tell her about his encounter with the traders and everything that had happened that night, from them trying to kill him, to Spartacus saving him, to Frederick giving him the knife. "And so I don't think you would attack me," Will concluded, "but I just can't be sure."

"Never mind then. I wouldn't give me the knife either if I were you. But I think I have a pretty strong mind, so it would take a lot of imps to make me do something," Liliu said, and then she turned her attention to Spartacus. "And you're the real hero, aren't you?"

Immediately enjoying the attention, Spartacus darted from Will's side to Liliu's.

"Yeah," Liliu continued in a baby voice while scratching Spartacus behind the ear. "You like me, don't you?"

"Yes, he does," Will answered for him.

"Where did you find him?"

"My dad's friend Cesar gave him to us when his dog had puppies," Will answered as he plucked a twisted brown stick from the ground. "He's been my best friend since." Will waved the stick in front of the dog to catch Spartacus's attention, and once he had it, he threw the stick as far as he could. Spartacus tore off after it.

"He seems great," Liliu said as she watched him snatch the stick at a full sprint and then turn and run back with it hanging out of both ends of his mouth.

"Yes, he is," Will said. Then he grabbed the stick, and after a short moment of tug-of-war, he pulled it free and hurled it back into the air. "So." Will paused. He wanted to find out about her parents but didn't know how to ask, so he decided to throw it out there and see what happened. "What happened to your parents—if you don't mind me asking?"

"No, I don't," Liliu replied as Will threw the stick again for Spartacus. "My mom died when she was giving birth to me."

"So did mine," Will said sympathetically.

"Yeah," Liliu said. "So my dad raised me, and he was a pickpocket himself—the best there ever was. He could pick your pocket while he was right there talking to you, and you would never know it. So he taught me everything about being a pickpocket. But we weren't bad people. He always told me to never take more than you need and never take from those that couldn't afford to lose a couple coins. So we tried to be nice about it."

"Nice pickpockets," Will said, smiling.

"That's right. And together, my dad and I—we were living pretty good. That is, until he caught the plague about two years ago." She suddenly paused and turned her head away from him. "He died on a Tuesday."

Will could see her try as casually as possible to wipe a tear away. He wanted to comfort her with a hand on her shoulder but decided not to. Spartacus, on the other hand, was not so shy; he attached himself to her leg, and she immediately began to stroke his fur.

"But that was a long time ago," she continued, shaking off her emotions. "Since then, I've been living on my own, picking whatever pocket I could to buy food or clothes. And really, I've been doing all right."

"So why did you decide to come with me?" Will asked, resuming his game of fetch with Spartacus.

"I'm tired of stealing. I want to do something that helps other people instead of just always helping myself."

"Well, you're helping me," Will said cheerfully.

"Thanks. Now it's my turn to ask the questions." But just as she said that, Will caught sight of Skyreach Forest. It was still in the distance, but there was no doubting why people called it Skyreach Forest; the trees were extraordinarily tall. Every single tree was a tower that stretched high into the air.

"Yeah, Skyreach Forest," Liliu said, staring at it as well. "You've never been there?"

"No," Will said, still a bit awestruck.

"Well, come on!" Liliu said, and then she burst into a fast jog. "Wait till you see it up close—it's amazing."

A smile erupted on Will's face, and he hurried after her. Spartacus decided this was a fun new game and began running between and around them with ease. Soon their jog turned into a sprint, which turned into a game of tag, and before they knew it, they were bent over in exhausted laughter at the border of the forest.

After finally catching his breath, Will looked up at the trees around him and marveled. The trunks of the giant trees were at least five feet thick and perfectly round, and the first branches didn't start until nearly fifty feet off the ground. The bark of the trees was a rich brown with tints of red. Besides the incredible size of the trees, their placement also amazed Will. The ground of the forest was perfectly flat, and each tree was given great space by the next so that their branches barely touched, which allowed thin wisps of sunlight to shower through. Between the trees, all along the ground, small ferns sprouted through a thin cover of grass.

"Wow," Will said in astonishment. "This place is amazing. Do you come here a lot?"

"Actually, I've only been here twice: once with my dad and once after he died."

"It sure is neat," Will said, still looking into the canopy. Then he shot his hand into his bag, pulled out the map that the king had given him, and unfolded it on the ground. "So we're right here," he said, pointing to a section labeled "Skyreach Forest" on the map, "and we need to get here." His finger slid up the map to Mount Inkedu. "That means the Witchwick Marshes are just ahead, and the king said that we should go around them."

"That'll take forever," Liliu said, scanning the size of the marshes on the map.

"Yeah, but it's better than running into witches."

"I guess so," Liliu acquiesced. "Then we should probably get moving, or by the time we get to the other side of the marshes, it will be too late—right?"

"Yeah. The Darkness isn't moving fast, but it never stops or has to rest."

Will packed up the map, and the two of them started into the forest. Spartacus was having a great time running off into the trees and then turning around and racing back to Will and Liliu.

"What's that?" Will asked, noticing for the first time that something was poking out from under Liliu's shirt.

Liliu reached back and pulled out a forked wooden stick with a handle and a rope tied to two of the ends, which she had tucked into the back of her pants. "My slingshot," she said, holding it up. "It's just a stick with some kind of special elfin rope tied to it."

"What does it do?" Will asked.

"It …" Liliu paused and began searching the ground. Then she said, "Watch this." Liliu quickly found a small stone, picked it up, and placed it in the rope of the slingshot, between her thumb and forefinger. She pulled the elfin rope back as far as it would go and released. The rock shot from the slingshot with incredible speed and bounced off two trees before it finally disappeared.

"Wow!" Will exclaimed. "Where did you find that?"

"My dad got it for me just before he died. It's come in handy."

"I bet."

"Okay," Liliu said, tucking her slingshot back in her pants, "now it's time for my questions."

Will nodded. He wanted to see the slingshot, but he realized it was special to her, so he decided not to ask. Besides, he was happy to continue talking to her. Now that he could talk to her calmly, he was starting to notice the small details that complemented her face, such as the lightly colored freckles that dotted her nose, and the dashes of green in her bright blue eyes.

"How come you got chosen to fight the Darkness?" she asked, and Will looked away quickly, hoping she hadn't noticed him staring.

"I don't know," Will said as he shrugged. "I was just playing with my friends, when I was told that the king wanted to talk to me. Then, the next thing I knew, they were telling me that I was the one in Voltaire's dream."

"Who?" Liliu asked.

"The king's personal wizard."

"Oh."

"Then they said that I would have an answer that would end the Darkness."

"An answer?" Liliu said incredulously.

"I know. I don't get it either."

"You mean you don't know what it is?" Liliu gasped.

"No. I have no idea," Will replied, and for a second, Liliu just stared at him.

"Are you sure you're the right one?"

"That's what I asked," Will said. "But the wizard said he was certain it was me."

Liliu continued on in silence, obviously pondering Will's situation. "Have you thought about what the question might be?"

"Yep, and I have no idea. I've decided I'm just gonna wait until I get asked the question rather than worry about all the things it could be. For all I know, the question could be 'How old is Spartacus?'"

Liliu waited for a second, but when Will didn't answer his own question, she asked it again. "So how old is he?"

"Almost four."

"Well, you'd better get more precise than that if that's the question that's gonna save everyone," Liliu joked.

"Three years, seven months, nineteen days, four hours, six minutes, and thirty-eight seconds," Will said as seriously as possible. "Is that better?"

"Much," Liliu said, and they both shared a laugh.

Side by side, they ventured deeper into Skyreach Forest. Will had to be sure that he kept a straight line north as much as possible, because the farther they went, the more everything looked the same. The forest seemed to maintain a kind of chaotic symmetry, so no matter where they looked, they saw the same huge trees. Fortunately, the openness allowed for fast travel, and before they knew it, they found themselves in the rancid smell of the marshes—the aroma was like decaying plants and rotting flesh.

"Oh," Liliu said in disgust. "Is that the marshes?"

"I think so."

"Well, now I'm glad we're going around. And maybe we shouldn't get so close."

"I'm not going to argue with that," Will said.

Just as they started to back up, a branch from high above fell and exploded into pieces in front of them. Both Liliu and Will shot their eyes to the canopy above. Will couldn't see anything, just long wooden branches; he was about to discount the incident as a coincidental break, but then Spartacus started to growl. "What is it, Spartacus?"

An eerie calm settled over the trees, and Will suddenly realized how quiet everything was in this forest. Without Liliu or his voice, there wasn't a sound at all. Then a flutter that Will couldn't see erupted from somewhere high up.

"That sounded like a big bird," Liliu said as her eyes darted from branch to branch.

"Maybe we should move a bit closer to the marshes, just for now," Will said as he absentmindedly started to back up.

"Okay," Liliu agreed with her eyes in the air.

As they walked, they got the impression they were being followed from somewhere high up. More small branches and needles began to fall from above and shower all around them. They started to walk faster, and the sounds of rustling branches got louder, until the three of them were jogging once again. The rancid smell of the marshes was growing stronger, but the marsh was still out of sight through the trees. Suddenly, from above, a creature with the body of a woman—but covered in giant golden feathers, with arms that were giant feathered wings and feet that were clawed talons—dropped from the canopy and swooped low across the forest floor. With its claws outstretched, it tried to snatch Spartacus away, but he dropped at the last instant, and the creature sailed over him. Will and Liliu had dropped to the ground themselves, and they watched the feathered beast glide back up into the trees.

"Harpies!" Liliu screamed.

Will was the first back to his feet, and he quickly drew his dagger. *This time, I will be ready,* he thought. Liliu was back up next, and she pulled out her slingshot. But neither of them wanted to fight, so again, they darted toward the marshes, this time at a full sprint. However, the bravery of that one harpy seemed to encourage the rest of them, and soon they were dropping from the trees like vultures to a carcass. Will, Liliu, and Spartacus found themselves weaving from side to side and sometimes dropping to their stomachs to keep from being yanked off the ground and pulled into the treetops. The high-pitched cries of the harpies bounced all around them as the excited creatures raged into a frenzy.

"Liliu!" Will yelled. He'd lost sight of her and was too busy dodging and weaving to look around. "Liliu!"

"I'm here!" she cried, and Will managed to catch a glimpse of her as she fired a small stone from her slingshot at one of the harpies, causing it to swerve and climb back into the air. "I'm okay—so far!"

Surprisingly, Spartacus seemed to be having the most trouble, as harpy after harpy dived for him. One managed to catch Spartacus's back leg, and he yelped as it lifted him into the air. Will sprinted toward him. Luckily, the harpy's grip failed, and Spartacus came crashing back down, but Will was there to catch him. He thudded heavily into Will's chest, knocking him to the ground, but Will managed to hang on, and they both landed unhurt. Recovering quickly, Will went on the offensive, slashing wildly with his dagger. The surprised harpies stumbled in the air, and a few of them crashed into one another and then tumbled to the ground. This was the window they needed.

"Run!" Will hollered, and the three of them were off again. Will could now see the marshes, and he hoped with all he had that the harpies would not follow them in.

As they sprinted, the calling of the harpies continued and grew closer. Their pursuers were getting close enough that Will could hear the flapping of their wings at his back. But before they could reach out and grab his shirt, Will hit the waters of the marsh behind Liliu and Spartacus. The moment his legs splashed into the cool green water, the harpies jetted upward. Crying out in frustration, they returned, squawking, to the treetops. Whatever was in the marshes, the harpies wanted nothing to do with it.

SIX

THE NIGHT ANACONDA

William and Liliu were standing in knee-deep marsh water that reeked of the vilest smells. They had turned and were watching the frustrated harpies flutter from tree to tree while calling out to one another as if blaming one another for their failure in acquiring a meal. Meanwhile, Spartacus was wandering around in the marshes, looking for the shallowest spot. He was eventually able to find a place where the water was only an inch or two deep.

"Liliu, are you okay?" Will asked as he watched Spartacus shake every bit of foul water from his coat, throwing hundreds of droplets of water into the air around him.

"Yeah, I'm fine. You?"

"I'm okay, and it looks like Spartacus is okay too."

"Well," Liliu said as she looked from the harpies, which were still fluttering about in the treetops, to the marshes and then to Will, "what do you want to do?"

"I'd rather not go through the marshes," Will said as he sloshed closer to Liliu. "Maybe we can walk along the edge of the marsh until the harpies give up on us."

"It's worth a try," Liliu said as she tucked her slingshot away. Then the three of them started sloshing through the muck. Luckily, around the edge of the marsh, the water stayed shallow, so Spartacus was able to keep up while remaining just inside the murky water. Liliu and Will, on the other hand, were in a bit deeper, which made walking difficult. With each step that Will took, he could feel his feet sink into the mud; at one point, he almost lost a shoe, but with the help of Liliu, he managed to pull it free. After an hour of travel, the harpies were still following them. They bounced from treetop to treetop along the forest's edge.

"Will, look out!" Liliu screamed, and Will turned just in time to see a harpy diving silently toward him. He had no choice but to dive into the water, and the harpy sailed over him, shrieking at its failure. Quickly, Will jumped back to his feet, expecting more attempts, but none came.

"They're getting desperate," Will said, scanning the forest.

"And the sun is getting low," Liliu added, and they both looked west. The sun was hovering just over the horizon.

"We won't be able to see them at night."

"Or hear them," Liliu added, "until they have us."

Will looked into the marsh. It was as eerie as he'd imagined. A low fog was starting to grow over the surface of the water, slowly devouring shoots of tall grass and the occasional twisted tree covered in dark-green moss. But worst of all, the fog seemed to go on forever in all directions except back toward the harpies.

"We have to go into the marsh," Will said more hopelessly than he wanted to.

"And what about the witches?" Liliu asked, keeping her eyes on the tree line.

Will had no answer for her. All he knew was that right now, taking their chances with the witches seemed to be better than their chances with the harpies, because only the harpies knew where they were. So he answered with a shrug and headed into the fog of the marsh.

A little more hesitant, Spartacus followed. The marsh was even more of a chore for him because the water was usually about chest high on him. There were times when it was shallower, but there were also times when it was deeper, and Spartacus found himself dog-paddling. After a while, William picked up his dog, seeing that he was already soaked himself, and carried him across the deepest areas, occasionally with Liliu's help. Spartacus never protested. He would just wait calmly in Will's arms and occasionally lick Will's face, no doubt in gratitude.

It didn't take long before the sounds of the harpies disappeared completely, along with the forest, as it was drowned out by the fog. Now that they were surrounded by the marsh, a creepy quiet settled around them. They heard no frogs, no crickets—nothing but the sounds of their own feet moving through the water.

"I don't like this place," Liliu whispered, and Spartacus concurred with a low whine.

"Still glad you decided to come with me?" Will joked, but Liliu did not laugh. "Well, I'm glad you're here," Will added, and he could see her blush even in the dim light of the marsh.

"We should probably start looking for some dry land, if there is any, so that we can get some sleep tonight," Liliu said, quickly changing the subject.

"Yeah," Will agreed, and he looked west to find the sun starting to disappear into distant dark water.

Liliu and Will began scanning for anything dry, but the search seemed hopeless. Everywhere Will looked, all he could find was water and mud. Only the tall grass seemed to be even partially dry. Then it hit him.

"Liliu, over there," Will said, pointing to a small island.

"That's all mud."

"Yeah, but if we cover it in enough grass, it should keep us dry enough to sleep on."

Liliu thought about the idea for a moment and then said, shrugging, "That's probably the best we're gonna find. Let's do it."

The two of them started pulling the long blades of grass from the water and laying them on the small island. Luckily, because there were so many grass shoots around, they were able to cover the island in a comfortable layer before the sun had totally disappeared. Then the three of them climbed on and took a seat.

With the disappearance of the sun, Will was starting to feel the chill of the marsh, especially because the front of him was still soaking wet from the dive he'd had to make earlier. Fortunately, Will was pleasantly surprised to find that the blanket he kept in the sack on his back was still dry, unlike his other shirt and jacket, which were as damp as he was. But before he threw the blanket around himself, he noticed Liliu shiver.

"Here," Will said, extending the blanket out to her.

"No," Liliu said. "You keep it. You're the one who's all wet."

"No, it's okay. I'm not even really cold," he lied, and then he placed the blanket at Liliu's feet.

"Thank you," Liliu said, and then she took the blanket and wrapped it around her shoulders.

Next, Will reached back into his bag and pulled out a couple of strips of salted beef and another one of those rock-hard rolls for Spartacus. "Are you hungry?" Will asked.

"Starving."

"Well, you're in luck," Will said, and he handed her a strip of the beef along with an apple.

"Thank you," she said gratefully, and she began devouring her food immediately.

"Wow," Will said, watching her attack her meal. "You are hungry."

Liliu smiled shyly but kept eating. Will tossed Spartacus a roll and a piece of beef and then began chowing down himself. Suddenly, the marsh was full of sounds of chomping and chewing. Occasionally, Will looked up to see Liliu smiling at him with a full mouth. He smiled back meekly and then quickly turned to Spartacus. He'd never wanted to talk so much, yet he couldn't think of anything to say. So he just ate instead. When they all finished, Liliu wiped the corners of her mouth with her hand and then held it out for Spartacus to lick clean.

"I needed that," she said.

"I think we all did," Will said, and then he took a moment to look up at the moon. It wasn't quite full, but it was doing a good job of adding an eerie white glow to the already-eerie marsh. Amazingly, the white light caught Liliu's blue eyes in a way that made them shine like blue crystals. Before he knew it, he was saying, "It's pretty tonight."

"Are you mad?" Liliu whispered in astonished disbelief.

"I mean," Will stammered, "the moon is pretty."

Liliu looked up, obviously humoring him. "I guess," she said, and then she returned her eyes to Will and started to smile. She suddenly seemed to understand his comment.

"Well, we should probably get some sleep," Will said before things could get any more awkward. "We can start traveling early. Maybe witches like to sleep in?"

Liliu laughed quietly and then lay down and wrapped herself tightly in Will's blanket. "Good night, Will."

Will watched her for a moment after she closed her eyes and then lay down himself with Spartacus at his side. As he closed his eyes and tucked his arm under his head, he got poked in the side. Reaching down, he found his dagger. Quietly, he removed it from his belt and placed it next to him so that if he needed it, he could grab it quickly. After a quick pat on Spartacus's head, he rolled over and closed his eyes. The night was cool, but there was no wind. Soon the exhaustion of the day caught up with Will, and he was fast asleep.

The Night Anaconda was a master of stealth. It glided across the waters of the marsh without a sound as its forked red tongue darted in and out of its mouth, tasting the air for a single scent—William's. The aroma was getting stronger. William's smell was emanating from a small, muddy island just yards from the Night Anaconda.

As it got closer, it slowed to a stalking pace. With the patience of a river as it wore at the rocks in its current, the snake edged forward an inch at a time. Careful to avoid the noisy grass, it used the length of its body to swerve around and between the patches of vegetation, creating a large S. Soon it was staring at William from only two feet away. He was fast asleep with a dog beside him. The Night Anaconda raised its large head into the air and then began winding itself around the edge of the grass pad that William had made. It would wrap the boy in its coils and squeeze him until no air remained in his lungs, and then it would crush him more until his bones were broken, allowing the Night Anaconda to devour him whole.

Starting at William's feet, the Night Anaconda slowly and gently began wrapping itself around his legs. Will was aware of nothing, and neither was the dog by his side. It continued on, skipping his body, because that would be sure to wake him; instead, it went to his neck. As it slid slowly under his chin, Will made a sound, and the snake froze. But fortunately, Will remained unconscious, so the Night Anaconda resumed slowly, wrapping itself once around his neck and then around his head. Then, meticulously, it began to bring its body up and around William's torso.

This, the snake knew, would surely wake him, but it was ready.

William felt a sudden chill on the back of his neck and a peculiar feeling of being lifted off the ground by some strange force. In fact, the snake's movements had been so slow and methodical that he opened his eyes with no urgency. In the darkness of the marsh, Will couldn't see anything, but as his mind became more aware, he tried to sit up—and suddenly realized that he couldn't move. Then everything became clear at once: he could see nothing because there was something in front of his eyes, and he couldn't move because there was something around his body.

Panic hit him, and he began jerking his muscles as hard as he could against the force that held him, but nothing moved. He couldn't move so much as an inch. He tried to yell, but his jaw was being held closed so that all that escaped was a low moan. Then the snake started to squeeze, and Will could feel his body being crushed. Will tried to scream again, and again, the sound came out as just a low moan, but this time, Spartacus heard him. Through the snake's coils, Will could hear Spartacus begin to bark and snarl. Then something moved around his eyes, and he could see what was holding him: a giant black snake.

Spartacus was barking wildly now and biting the anaconda's tough skin, but his teeth weren't sharp enough to penetrate it. Fortunately, the commotion had awakened Liliu, and she was up in a flash. Searching frantically, she managed to find a thick, soggy stick, which she used to pummel the snake, but it did no good. After only a few strikes, the stick broke into several pieces, and Liliu was reduced to kicking the snake, which wasn't doing much either. Will wanted to scream out and tell her to take the dagger by his side, but his lungs were compressed, and his mouth was covered. Then, just as a sharp pain cut across his side, Will saw Spartacus begin digging for something under the snake. He was sure Spartacus was going for the dagger. Another sharp pain cut into him. Will could feel his ribs begin to bend slightly. If they didn't stop the snake soon, his body was going to be crushed.

From between the snake's coils, Will spotted Liliu drop to her knees beside Spartacus. She had figured out what he was digging for. A second later, she yanked the dagger from under the black snake, pulled it from its sheath, and plunged the blade into the snake's body.

Will could feel the snake loosen instantly. Although it wasn't dead, it was hurt, and Will's head was released so that the snake could bring its own diamond-shaped head to a fighting position. But as soon as it did, Spartacus lunged for its throat. With a solid bite, he brought the snake's head to the ground—but only momentarily, as the powerful creature was able to shake him off, sending Spartacus twirling into the marsh. But that moment was all the distraction Liliu needed, and she threw herself at the snake with a desperate swing of the dagger. In the dim light, Will saw the blade cut through the anaconda's jaw, and then he heard the skull crunch as the dagger was pushed through the creature's head. Shaking wildly, the snake began convulsing in the air. Black blood ran down the handle of the dagger. As the snake's grip loosened more and more, Will started squirming out of its coils. Fighting with the scales, Will brought himself to his feet as quickly as he could and then stumbled back away from the creature. After a few last furious convulsions, the snake's head dropped lifelessly to the ground. Will, Liliu, and Spartacus huddled together with their eyes locked on the lifeless serpent.

"Will, are you okay?" Liliu asked, her eyes still locked on the snake's dead body.

Will took a few deep breaths. His sides were sore, but there didn't seem to be any damage. "I think so," he finally answered. Then he felt Spartacus's wet tongue kissing his face.

"Seems like Spartacus is happy to hear that you're okay too," Liliu said, and Will forced a smile. Normally, Will would have laughed, but laughter wasn't in him right now.

"I didn't know this kingdom had snakes like that," Liliu said, staring at the giant reptile.

"Yeah," Will said absentmindedly, and then he added in a whisper, "I don't know if it does."

"What do you mean?"

"Well, this is the second time something has tried to kill me since I have left on this journey. I just think ..." Will's voice trailed off. He wasn't sure he wanted to say any more. He didn't want to scare Liliu off—or scare himself, for that matter.

"You think it was the Darkness?"

"I don't know," Will said reluctantly, still unable to take his eyes off the snake. "But Voltaire told me that it could take any form."

Liliu looked at him for a long moment. He was waiting for her to tell him that she was going to go back to Potemkin Village in the morning, but suddenly, she smiled and said, "Well, then you've already beaten the Darkness twice."

After hearing that, Will had to smile back. That was exactly what he'd needed to hear.

"Thanks," he said, and Liliu picked up the blanket, sat down, and offered a section of it to Will. Gratefully, he sat next to her—but only for a second, because a moment later, Spartacus inched his way between them. Huddled together, they all fell asleep.

SEVEN

WITCHES OF WITCHWICK

A cool morning chill swept across Will's face as the sun's rays began to glow over the horizon. Will had managed to sleep a bit more, but it had been a fragile sleep that broke whenever there was the slightest noise. Fortunately, they had managed to keep warm while huddled so close, which meant that Will's shirt was dry by dawn, a welcome feeling. Looking lazily to his side, he saw Liliu's eyes wide open.

"I suppose we should get going," Will said reluctantly, half hoping that Liliu would object.

Will watched as she slowly brought herself to her feet and walked cautiously toward the giant anaconda.

"What are you doing?" Will asked.

Liliu didn't answer; she just stepped a little closer, gave it a swift kick, and jumped back. Will and Spartacus watched the snake closely for any movement, but there was none. So Liliu started to approach once again.

"Liliu, what are you doing?" Will asked again anxiously.

"I'm getting the dagger," Liliu answered as she reached for the handle covered in thick black blood. But when she tried to pull it out, her hand slipped, and she nearly fell back into Will's lap. "It's stuck," she said as she wiped her hands in the grass and grabbed the handle again, this time placing her foot on the snake's large head. However, as she pulled, her hand slid down the handle and then off and into the air. "My hands are too slippery. Do you think you can get it?" she said, turning to Will.

Hesitantly, Will stood and made his way to the black serpent's body.

"Don't worry," Liliu said. "It's dead."

Will nodded and placed his foot on the beast's head; then he grabbed the handle and started to pull. The blade was in there good. Will had to take the handle with his other hand and pull with all his might. Suddenly, the handle came free, and Will stumbled back. He tripped over Spartacus and fell back into the shallow marsh water. Once again, William was wet.

Liliu threw both of her hands over her mouth in an attempt not to laugh and then quickly gathered her wits and ran to his side to help him up.

"I'm sorry, Will," she said as she took his hand and pulled him to his feet.

"At least I got the dagger," Will said grouchily, but when he looked down, all he saw was the handle. The blade had broken off in the snake. In frustration, Will let out a groan and hurled the handle as far as he could into the mist of the marsh. A splash followed a moment later, and he snatched his bag from the ground and stuffed his blanket back into it.

"Let's go," Will said in an agitated tone, and Liliu patted him on the back as he passed. Then the three of them were off once again, marching through the water.

The morning was cold and damp. It seemed that no matter how high the sun got, the temperature stayed the same, which was not helping Will dry off. Wet and irritable, he trudged on. Even Spartacus seemed down. His tail and head were both low as he navigated the shallowest regions of the marsh.

Liliu seemed to have the highest spirits of the three, but even she was silent. In fact, nobody said anything for an hour. The only sounds were those of their feet sloshing through the water and mud. Just ahead, they discovered an odd-looking tree with a huge trunk that arched out of the water like the neck of a giant dragon before it dived back into the mud and then twisted up into a tangled mess of branches and moss.

"Is everybody else as hungry as I am?" Will asked as he slipped his bag from his shoulder and plopped himself down on the large tree.

"Hungry and tired," Liliu said, sitting beside him. Spartacus jumped up onto the trunk, which was thick enough to allow him to sit comfortably as well.

William pulled out some beef, which he gave in plenty to Spartacus. "Thanks for saving me again, buddy." And then he pulled out an apple and gave it to Liliu. "This is my last apple. Thanks for helping Spartacus," Will half joked, and Liliu took it with a smile.

"We'll split it," she told him. She took a huge bite and handed it back to Will.

"Do you think there are really witches around?" Will asked before he bit into the apple.

Liliu started to take in the scenery around her before saying, "If I were a witch, this is where I would want to live."

William let out a small laugh that he felt he had to force. The marshes seemed to be sucking the happiness out of him. "We need to get out of here," Will said, taking another big bite out of the apple and then continuing with a full mouth. "I don't like this place."

"Me neither," Liliu concurred. "Hopefully we'll get through it by this afternoon."

"Yeah," Will said. Then he turned to a tired Spartacus, who looked exactly like they all felt. "Ready, Spartacus?"

His loyal companion stood reluctantly and jumped back

into the mud and water. Liliu took the last bite of the apple and tossed the core into the mist. Together, the tired group pushed on. As tired and down as Will was, he knew that he could not let the despair win, so he focused on his gratitude for his friends, both new and old. He could not have made it this far without them.

The marsh was unrelenting. Will, Liliu, and Spartacus continued on through the afternoon, and there was no sign of the marsh coming to an end. They saw only more black water beneath an eerie white mist that seemed to cling to their skin, keeping it clammy and cold. Yet Will was not ready to give up. He pushed himself and his friends on into the dusk until the last of the light was about to vanish. Only then was he willing to give in and settle for another night in the marsh.

William and Liliu did as they had done the previous night and covered a small, muddy island with grass. Then Will retrieved his blanket, and the three of them huddled together. Will and Liliu were pressed back-to-back, with Spartacus curled up next to Will. Amazingly, William was warm for the first time all day. As he warmed, he tired. Soon his eyelids felt as though they each weighed a hundred pounds, and the next thing he knew, he was asleep.

It seemed as if his eyes had just closed when he felt an elbow nudging him in the side. Annoyed and grumpy, Will turned to face Liliu. "What?"

Liliu didn't say a word; she just pointed in front of her. Will followed her finger and found a small sparkle of red light bouncing along a little way into the mist.

"What is it?" Will whispered.

"I don't know," Liliu answered, and the two of them remained frozen as the light slowly drew nearer, zipping around, seemingly at random.

Will heard a light whine and realized that Spartacus had

seen it too. "Shhh," Will said softly, and Spartacus quieted instantly.

The sparkle of light continued to bounce closer until it was just feet from the three of them. It seemed that the closer it got, the less Will breathed, until it was right on him, and he stopped breathing altogether. Then, suddenly, it made a noise like a tiny bell and shot off behind them as straight as an arrow.

"I have a bad feeling about this," Liliu said as she watched the critter disappear into the distant mist.

"Me too," Will said, and he forced himself to his feet. "I think we should go."

"I'm not gonna argue with that."

Quickly, Liliu stuffed the blanket into Will's bag as he held it open, and then they started north at a fast pace, kicking noisily through the shallow water.

"Shhh," Liliu said urgently, and Will froze alongside Spartacus. "Listen." In the silence of the marsh, the faintest laughter could be heard, but it wasn't jolly by any means. It was a laughter that made the hair on the back of Will's neck stand on end. It was a cackling that could only come from a witch. And then it happened again and again. "Witches. Lots of them!"

Will couldn't stop himself; he broke into a sprint with the others right behind him. He didn't care how noisy he was now; he just wanted to get out of the marsh. But the laughter got louder the harder he ran, and then a shadowy figure on a wooden broom whooshed by him. Immediately, Will thought about the dagger but quickly remembered that it was gone. Then two more witches glided in above him, crowing loudly to each other.

"Hello, dearies," one of them screeched, and soon four others were around them.

Two witches were up front, with two above and four more

to their sides and rear, all with pointy black hats and long dark robes, gliding effortlessly on old straw brooms.

"Will, don't stop!" Liliu yelled, and Will pushed on as hard as he could with his already-fatigued muscles.

"Yes, Will," one of the witches mocked. "Don't stop, Will! Don't stop!" Then, with a scream, she began cackling wildly.

Spartacus was doing his best to appear fierce, occasionally barking and growling, but Will could tell that the dog was just as tired as he and Liliu were. Will didn't know how much longer he could keep running, and worse, he knew that fleeing was futile anyway. The witches had them and were just playing with them. However, Will did have one weapon left: the crystal that the dragon had given him. He could feel it in his pocket and knew that all he had to do was break it, and the dragon would come. So with no hope left, Will placed the crystal between his fingers and pushed the middle with his thumb—but it wouldn't break. It was much harder than the dragon had made it seem when he had so easily plucked it from his own body. Again, Will pushed on it with his thumb, and again, it didn't so much as crack.

"Run, Will," the witches said, continuing to mock him as they sailed by him. "Run! Run!"

Will was too tired to run anymore and was about to turn and fight, when he heard a loud splash behind him. Stopping as quickly as he could, he spun around and saw Liliu facedown in the mud. "No!" Will screamed, and he ran to her side, but before he got to her, something struck him in the back of the head, and everything went black.

A sharp pain snapped Will out of unconsciousness, and his eyes opened to the pointed yellow teeth and pale-green skin of a witch's face as she poked him with the tip of her broom. When she saw Will's eyes open, she began cackling ecstatically and then turned and scurried off to join the others. It took a second for Will to realize where he was, but it soon became clear: he was in a wooden prison. There were wooden bars on all sides of him, including the top and bottom, making sitting uncomfortable, but the cage wasn't tall enough for Will to stand in; he had to either stoop or sit. Looking outside of the cage, Will could tell that he was still in the marsh. The ground was muddy, and the witches had used the mud to make short, round huts with matted grass roofs. All around the small witch village were torches that lit the area in flickering orange light that seemed to keep the mist away. Next to Will in a separate wooden cage was Liliu, still unconscious, and below her was Spartacus, who was sitting uncomfortably in his own cage. Beside Spartacus, in an even smaller cage, was a dark-green frog that seemed to be looking back at him with an expression of compassion. The witches were gathered in the center of the village around a long wooden table and were excitedly going through Will's bag.

Seeing that, panic suddenly set in, and Will felt his pocket. The crystal was gone. Hoping with all his heart that the witches hadn't taken it, he began frantically searching the ground below him. The cages were built a few feet off the ground, so even if Will did find it, he wouldn't be able to get to it. But he didn't care; he just wanted to make sure that the witches didn't have it or that he hadn't dropped it when he was carried there. His eyes scanned anxiously, yet he didn't see anything, and his heart began to sink. Then, just as he was about to give up, he caught sight of a tiny red gleam— it was the crystal. Relief swept over Will; even though he couldn't get to it, he knew where it was.

Slowly and groggily, Liliu started to come to. Will let her find her wits before he whispered, "Liliu, are you okay?"

"I think so," she answered. "Where are we?"

"I think we're in a witch village."

Liliu took a moment to look around and then turned back to Will. "What are they doing?"

"Going through my bag," Will said, scowling at them.

Liliu suddenly felt behind her. "My slingshot is gone!"

"The witches probably have it," Will said, and then he turned his attention to the cage. "We need to get out of here."

Liliu began examining her prison. Her eyes scanned the twine that held the edges together and the knots that looked as if they could also be the hinges. Reaching out, she tested the sturdiness of the structure with a shake, and Will did the same.

"They may look flimsy," Will said, giving one of his wooden bars another yank, "but they're strong."

"Every cage has a door, and every door has a lock," Liliu replied, still scanning. "I found it," she said, pointing to a thick wooden ring that looped out of a gray stone. "All I need now is some kind of pick; anything will do," she said, looking around again.

"What about this?" Will said as he pulled a splinter from one of his bars.

"It might be a little weak, but it's worth a try," Liliu said. Then she took the sliver from Will and began looking for the lock's keyhole. Meanwhile, Will kept an eye on the witches.

After several moments of searching, Liliu whispered, "I can't find it."

"Find what?"

"The keyhole," Liliu said, confused.

"That's because there isn't one," a voice said from the small cage next to Spartacus.

Liliu and Will shot their eyes to the frog, but it had stopped talking, if it had spoken at all.

"Did you say something?" Will asked slowly, not sure what to expect. To his surprise, the frog answered.

"Of course I did. I said there is no keyhole."

"Well then, how do the witches lock it?" Liliu asked, clearly a little surprised that she was talking to a frog.

"With magic, of course," the frog answered.

"Then how do we unlock it?" Liliu asked, more to herself than to the frog.

"We don't," the frog said.

"Every lock can be picked," Liliu argued.

"Not these," the frog replied. "Not unless you know magic."

"We don't know any magic," Will said. He wasn't sure if Liliu knew any or not, but he was pretty sure she didn't, and he saw that he was right, because she was shaking her head at their fellow prisoner.

"Then we are all trapped—until the witches decide to eat us," the frog said hopelessly, and Spartacus whined.

"Who are you?" Will asked. He was surprised to see the dark-green frog perk up at the question.

"I am Fyodor Dostoevsky," he said while standing on his hind legs, as if announcing his name to a grand audience. "The greatest swordsman the world has ever seen." Then he slunk back down to a frog's four-legged posture and added much more quietly, "Or so I used to be."

"What happened to you?" Liliu asked.

"Ahh," the frog said, standing once again, "that is an epic tale worthy of the greatest author; however, I will tell it in its humblest form. I was a guardian of the king himself—"

"King Herodotus?" William couldn't help but ask.

"Yes, King Herodotus," Fyodor answered gloriously. "I have battled for His Majesty's safety many times and have never faltered. However, as it was, upon my fortieth birthday, for my great and honorable service to the king, they retired my sword. Of course, I did not want to leave, but it was the way of things, and so I submitted to tradition. Two years and four months ago, I packed my things and left the castle. For a time, I traveled this great kingdom, but I quickly decided that it was time to settle down. And so I built a cottage just there"—Fyodor pointed a long, webbed finger back into the marsh—"beyond the edge of the marsh."

Will and Liliu traded a look that Will knew meant they should have just kept walking for another hour, for if they had, they never would have been in this mess.

"There," Fyodor continued, "I lived in peace for the past year—until recently, that is. I was tending my garden, when I heard a group of kids—no doubt traders' children—venture into the marsh. I knew there would be trouble, so I retrieved my sword and fell in pursuit. And just as I had guessed, the moment the children entered this grotesque region of the kingdom, they were snatched up by those vile witches." Fyodor paused for a moment to scowl at the cloaked creatures still going through Will's things. They had obviously decided that the salted beef was gross and not worth eating. "So being the hero that I was, I charged into this treacherous encampment with my sword ready, and it was a glorious battle! Fighting with every bit of guile that I possessed, I managed to free the children and had the witches on the run—until I was struck by this horrible curse. One of the older witches attacked me from behind, and so I awoke as the creature you see before you, locked in this wooden prison." With those final words, Fyodor sank back onto four legs and gazed longingly out into the marsh beyond.

"Did the kids get away?" Will asked, unsure if the frog had already said.

"Yes," Fyodor answered. "My transformation was not in vain."

"How long have you been here?" Liliu asked.

"One entire moon as of tonight," Fyodor said, looking up at the full moon, which was passing behind a wisp of clouds.

"And now," he added solemnly, "all that's left of who I was is my sword."

Will followed his gaze to a silver hilt protruding from a pile of mud and twigs. Will felt sorry for him. He couldn't imagine what it would be like to be turned into a frog. But Fyodor had been there for a month; he must know something that could help them.

"Fyodor," Will said, "how can we escape? There must be some way out of these cages."

"There is not," he replied sorrowfully. "I'm afraid you two are doomed."

"I will not accept that," Liliu said. "Nothing is hopeless. Now, what do you know about the witches that can help us?"

Fyodor thought for a moment and then said, "They lose their powers during the day, but at night, they are quite formidable."

"So we have to last the night," Liliu said optimistically.

"Do you know what time it is?" Will asked.

"I do not," Fyodor answered. "But dawn cannot be too far away."

"Fyodor, can you fit through the bars of your cage?" Liliu asked.

Fyodor looked bleakly at his wooden bars and then back up at Liliu. "I think not."

"Well, have you tried?" Liliu pressed.

"No, I haven't, but what use would there be if I did escape? I am only a frog; there is nothing that I can do for you now."

"You could get my crystal," Will whispered, and Liliu shot him a curious look. "The red crystal below me; if I break it, a dragon will come."

"What?" said Liliu in surprise. "Why didn't you break it earlier?"

"I tried, but it was too hard to break with my fingers. But I'm sure that I can break it with two hands."

Liliu shot a look back at Fyodor, who was looking at them incredulously. "Fyodor, can you try to fit through the bars? Will needs that crystal."

Fyodor seemed to take a moment to measure the situation, but before he could speak, the witches began cackling once again, and two of them started over toward the cages.

"Hmmm," one of them screeched. "Which one should we eat tonight?"

"The dog looks mighty tasty," the other said, wiggling her fingers with long dark nails at Spartacus. "But I'm in the mood for the flesh of a boy tonight."

Both of them started laughing as they approached Will's cage. Then one of them took his lock into her hand and whispered something into it, and it unlatched. As soon as the door swung open, Will dived out of the cage and tried to grab the crystal beneath it, but he was pulled away by two witches. With a leg in each hand, they dragged him effortlessly to a wooden table next to a large black caldron, where they were boiling a thick green goo. Several other witches gathered around the old wooden table and assisted in holding Will down. He struggled with all his might, but they were surprisingly strong and seemed to be holding him down with ease. Then another witch appeared, and this one had a large, rusty cleaver.

"So what should we eat first?" the one holding the cleaver asked. "His arms?" she said, pretending to cut them off. "His legs?" She mimicked the same gesture. "Or perhaps his head?" And with that, the whole group broke into laughter.

"His head, sister! His head!" one of them cried. The one with the cleaver reared back, and the witches roared with laughter. But just before she brought the cleaver down on William's throat, another witch, who was dressed in black like all the others, came racing out of her hut.

"Stop!" she screamed. "Stop!"

Obviously confused, the witches' cackling died down, and the witch with the cleaver slowly lowered the blade.

"This boy is William Locke!" the witch shouted, and the others gasped.

"Oh, for joy," one of them shrieked. "Now we can give him to the Darkness, and the Darkness will spare us."

The witches suddenly broke into a hurricane of laughter.

"Come now, sisters. Let's remove his head and present it to the Darkness."

"No!" one of them said urgently. "We must present him alive to the Darkness. That is how the Darkness will want it."

"Wrong!" another said scathingly. "The Darkness will want him dead—in pieces even!"

Suddenly, there was a storm of arguing, and one of the witches pulled Will off the table and held him securely behind her. No matter how hard he fought, the witch didn't budge. He was amazed at their strength. But now at least he could see his companions. Spartacus was gnawing at his bars and was about to chew through one of them, while Liliu was shouting at Fyodor.

"Fyodor, Will needs you. Push yourself through the bars!"

"I am but a frog, girl. I can do nothing in this form!"

"You can get the crystal before they kill him!" Liliu screamed, and Will expected a witch to look over, but they were so busy arguing that none of them took notice.

"Very well. I shall do what I can in this pathetic form," Fyodor said, and with a new determination, he drove his head between the bars. His flexible bones squished between the bars, and with one push after another, he inched his way out of the cage until his torso slipped through, and he went flying out to the ground below. Obviously a bit amazed that he had done it, Will watched him as he leaped under the cage that Will had been in and retrieved the red crystal. But before the frog could start hopping toward him, Will pointed at Liliu and lipped the words, "Break it." Stretching as high as he could, Fyodor handed the crystal to Liliu. Then, with all her might, she pressed her fingers against it, but it would not even crack. Desperately, she looked out at Will, who mouthed, "Keep trying."

Just then, Spartacus broke free from his cage and charged at the witches. Some of the witches noticed the snarling dog immediately and fled in all directions, while others jumped on top of the table, and still others stood their ground. Spartacus went for the ones that started to run, growling and barking as they scattered.

Will struggled desperately against the witch who was holding him, but again, she wouldn't give. Helplessly, he watched Liliu unsuccessfully try to break the crystal. Then he caught sight of Fyodor. He was standing on his two long hind legs and watching as Spartacus terrorized the witches, and suddenly, Will could see a change in him. Standing as erect as possible, the frog hollered loudly enough for all to hear, "I am Fyodor Dostoevsky! I fear nothing!"

With that, he leaped into the air and landed just feet from Will. Above him were the strongest witches, who hadn't run from Spartacus and had stood their ground with wands ready, firing curse after curse at Spartacus as he darted in and around huts, chasing witches indiscriminately. With finesse, Fyodor leaped over Will and over the witch who was holding him, and as he came down, he snatched the wand from another witch's hand. Then, standing on the table with the wand in his right webbed hand, he stood at the ready, as though he were about to start a fencing duel.

"On guard!" he roared, and one of the witches turned to him with a curse, but Fyodor deflected her wand, and the streak of red-and-gold light struck one of her sisters, turning her into a swarm of fireflies that buzzed off in all directions. With a scream, the witch tried again, and again, Fyodor parried. Then another witch fired a curse at the frog, but he was ready. He jumped high into the air with a back flip, and the curse sailed past him and struck the witch he had just been dueling with, turning her into stone. With his stolen wand ready, he began what looked like a fencing match; as the witch tried to curse him, Fyodor blocked and parried her every attempt, sending all the other witches running and ducking the stray curses.

The witch who was holding Will was not so lucky. She tried to run with Will still in her grasp, but Will did all he could to slow her down, and it worked. A blue-green curse struck her in the back, turning her into water that splashed to the ground. Without hesitating, Will jumped to his feet and dashed for Fyodor's sword. He grabbed the hilt, pulled the long silver blade from its muddy sheath, and then ran over to Liliu, who held out the crystal. Will snatched it from her hand and slid it into his pocket. He didn't want to use the dragon now; there was a chance that they could get out of this mess on their own.

"Stand back," Will ordered, and Liliu backed up against the rear of the cage. With a mighty swing, he cut the lock in half, and Liliu climbed out. Next thing he knew, Spartacus was at his side, and Will spun around. The witches had reorganized, and Fyodor was retreating to where Will and his friends were. A moment later, they were all together, surrounded by the remaining witches.

"You are luckier than we thought," one of the witches snarled. "But now we will kill your friends and take your head to the Darkness. No more chances." The witch curled her lips to reveal her pointy yellow teeth and then raised her wand, but when she thrust it toward Liliu, nothing happened. In the commotion, a single beam of light had broken over the horizon and touched Liliu's face, protecting her against the witch's power.

"Nooo!" the witch screamed. "Then we will kill you with our bare hands."

The witch lunged forward, but Will raised his sword, and she halted instantly.

"Do not touch her," Will commanded in a voice that surprised him, and the witch backed away, scowling.

"Come," Fyodor told them. "I know where to go."

With Fyodor walking gracefully on two feet in the lead, the group of four cautiously pushed through the crowd of witches and left the village. Will quickly retrieved Liliu's slingshot and the potion he had purchased in Potemkin Village but left everything else. He couldn't trust anything else the witches had handled. On his way out, Will saw the witches watching him with looks of pure malevolence. Luckily, they were only an hour's journey to the edge of the marsh, but Will kept his eye on the mist behind them the entire time. No witch would ever surprise him again.

EIGHT

FYODOR'S COTTAGE

A huge wave of relief hit William the moment he stepped from the soggy marsh to the expanse of dry land in front of him. The air was already much warmer, and the pine trees around him seemed like old friends. Spartacus's tail was wagging furiously, and Liliu was giggling, as it kept batting her leg. Fyodor, who had kept the witch's wand, decided he had no more need for it, so with his two webbed hands, he pulled it across the front of his right shin, breaking it in half. Then he tossed the pieces over his shoulder and into the water. Finally, the horrible marshes were behind them.

"We are not far now," Fyodor said, pointing straight ahead. "Only another few minutes and we'll be at my cottage. But, my friends, I'm afraid you have not introduced yourselves."

Will felt a bit ashamed and apologized, looking down at his new companion. Then he said, "My name is William, and this is Liliu." Will gestured to her, and she gave a tired wave. "And that is Spartacus." Spartacus looked up at Will briefly and then went back to sniffing the ground.

"Good to make your acquaintance," Fyodor said, but they were too tired to reply or hold any kind of conversation, for that matter. Their walk through the forest was a quiet one. Soon they came to a small structure in a tiny meadow with four simple walls and a pointed roof. The short side facing east had a tall burgundy door, while the longer sides had perfectly square windows.

"Your cottage is adorable," Liliu said.

"Thank you," Fyodor replied. "I think."

Will was the first to the door, and Fyodor hopped up onto a stump next to the house.

"Please go in," Fyodor said, and Will turned the fancy metal handle and entered. The place was quaint, with a simple bed, dresser, and chair at one side and a woodstove with a cupboard for cookware and a dining table at the other. However, as humble as the home was, it managed to maintain a kind of ostentatious feel with the number of medals and trophies mounted on every wall. The awards were the first thing to catch Will's attention.

"Wow," Will said as his eyes scanned the room. "Are these all yours?"

"Of course they are," Fyodor replied, jumping in the door and onto his bed and then the dresser. "All under the king's service."

Will wanted to ask about each one, but his tired mind did not have the patience, so he walked lethargically to the cushioned chair and dropped into it with a thud. Liliu was right behind him. She lowered herself a bit more gracefully onto the bed and then leaned back against the wall.

"Fyodor," Will said, still holding his beautiful silver sword, "where do you want me to put this?"

"Next to you is fine, young sir, but please leave the hilt off the ground."

Will followed his instructions exactly; stretching back, he placed the blade against the cupboard behind him, with the hilt at the top. Then he sank back into the chair.

"You are all exhausted and reasonably so," Fyodor said. "Please, rest now. We will talk once you have all had a chance to sleep."

Will did not need to be told twice. As his heavy eyelids closed, the last thing he saw was Spartacus waiting at the door and Fyodor waving him in.

"Please, my friend," Fyodor said. "You deserve to come in as much as I do."

Will heard Spartacus enter and felt him curl up at his feet. The next thing he knew, he was fast asleep.

Will awoke to the smell of seasoned chicken cooking in a woodstove. Bringing his hand to his face, he started to wipe away the sleepiness but ended up wiping away the drool on his chin. He noticed that Liliu was no longer in the bed next to him, so he stood with a tremendous stretch.

"Well, look who's finally awake," Liliu said from behind him.

Turning around, Will saw her standing over the stove with a pan that she had obviously just pulled from the oven. Inside it was a whole chicken, glowing with golden-brown skin. Now Will knew why he had been drooling.

Still a little too groggy to say anything, Will wandered outside, where he found Spartacus playing in the meadow. Will quickly located a stick and called to his friend, who darted over instantly. With a pat on his dog's head, Will threw the stick as far as he could, and Spartacus was off. After snatching the stick before it stopped tumbling, he darted back to Will to do it again.

"The chicken's done, if you're ready to start eating," Liliu said as she stepped beside him.

"I'm starving," Will replied, smiling at her. "That sounds great. Did you cook everything yourself?"

"Not really," Liliu said humbly. "Fyodor told me what to do."

"Well, thank you for doing everything."

"You're welcome," Liliu said. "Now, come on—let's eat. I'm starving too."

Will took a seat at the table, which had been set for three with a feast in the middle. There were chicken, green beans, and mashed potatoes, all steaming hot. Like the gentleman that his dad had taught him to be, Will served Liliu first and then turned to Fyodor, who held up a webbed hand.

"No, thank you, sir. As much as I would like to join you in this well-prepared meal, it seems that since my transformation, I no longer have an appetite for chicken." Fyodor paused for a moment, almost as though he were ashamed. "It seems that now all I enjoy are bugs."

Will and Liliu looked at each other and then back to Fyodor.

"I know," he continued, "but it's true. The bigger and juicer, the better."

Will felt his appetite starting to slip away.

"But I'm sure you don't want to hear about that," Fyodor said, as if reading Will's mind. "I am just here to enjoy your company."

With a smile and a nod, Will finished serving himself, and they began to feast. As Will and Liliu ate, Fyodor leaped around the room, regaling them with tales of how he had been awarded each of the many medals, from sword fights with giant, ugly ogres to duels with cunning assassins plotting against the king. As Will listened to all his stories, it became clear that Fyodor was proud of his service to the king. But after telling the story of his last medal, he slunk into a defeated posture and suddenly couldn't look either of them in the eye.

"But how can I ask you to believe such tales after the cowardice and ill spirit I showed last night?"

Will and Liliu looked at each other again, both a bit confused.

"If it weren't for you," Will said, putting down his fork, "the witches might have killed me last night."

"Yeah," Liliu agreed. "You were amazing last night."

"No," Fyodor countered, shaking his large green head. "It was you who were amazing. I had given up. I had surrendered to the wickedness of life. But it was your motivation, Liliu, and your bravery, William, that inspired me to great measures. However, what really cast me out of the depth of my despair was your noble dog, Spartacus. He charged into battle just as I used to do, and he is a dog. Not a man," Fyodor reiterated triumphantly, "but a dog! And that's when I realized that it is the spirit of a creature and not his form that makes him great, so all of you have my eternal gratitude."

Will patted Spartacus on the head and then raised his mug with Liliu to their new companion and drank. Fyodor humbly bowed.

"Now, please, William," Fyodor said politely, "tell me your story, as it seems that you have quite a tale yourself."

Will took the last bite off his plate, chewed it patiently, and then swallowed. He had decided a long time ago that this strange but noble frog was someone he wanted with him on his journey. He decided that he was only supposed to leave Castle Village alone, because of the first night, but now his companions were saving his life rather than trying to take it. After a deep breath, Will told Fyodor about everything: the Darkness, the Millennium Stone, and his journey.

Fyodor listened patiently, and at the end of the story, he humbly asked, "May I join you on your quest?"

"You may," Will said, and for some reason, all of them began laughing. Perhaps it was out of relief, a knowledge that this was a team brought together by fate to fight the Darkness, and they were ready.

After dinner, Will returned to his chair, and he was about to plop down in it once again, when he heard Fyodor call him.

"William?" Will had to look around for a moment to find him. And it was no wonder; he was on the floor beside his long silver sword. "I would like for you to have this sword. It has been a terrific weapon and is one worthy of your quest."

Will didn't know what to say; he was honored that Fyodor would give the sword to him, so he took it graciously. "Thank you, Fyodor. I won't mistreat it."

"I know you will not," Fyodor said confidently, "or I would not have offered it to you. Its sheath and belt are over there. They may be a little loose but are manageable."

Will placed the sword gently in its sheath and then placed the belt around his waist. Fyodor was right—it was a little loose. In fact, if it were any looser, the sword would have been dragging on the ground. Will did feel, however, a certain amount of confidence in placing the blade on his hip. Now he was ready for anything.

"Thank you again, Fyodor; this is great!" Will said, smiling, and then he turned to Liliu. "What do you think?"

"You look like a champion," she said, passing by him. Then she took a seat on the bed.

"A champion indeed," Fyodor concurred. Then he stood up and strolled out the door, patting Spartacus on his way out.

"Well, I'm gonna go back to sleep," Liliu said, rubbing her face. "I didn't get to sleep all day."

"Have a good night, and thanks again for dinner."

Liliu mumbled, "You're welcome," and then rolled over and started to drift off to sleep. Soon Fyodor joined her. Will placed a pillow on top of the dresser for him, which he had accepted gratefully. Will, on the other hand, having slept all day, wasn't tired, but he had an idea of what he was going to do with his time. He opened the dresser quietly and pulled out a metal knitting needle he had noticed earlier, and then he took it outside with a file that he found under the bed and a knife sharpener that was in the cupboard. Will wanted to return the gift he had so charitably been given.

Even though Will was the last to bed, he was the first to wake up. Even Fyodor was still fast asleep, curled up on his pillow. Will stood quietly, crept to the door, and opened it to see the first rays of the sun barely pushing through the pine trees. He had no doubt as to why Fyodor had chosen this location—it was beautiful. More than anything, Will wanted to stay one more day at the quaint cottage, but he knew there wasn't time. The Darkness was approaching, and if he didn't stop it, it would destroy everything. Then the daunting task of having the answer to some obscure question leaped back into his head. He was more than halfway through his journey but still hadn't a clue what answer he was supposed to know. Then it hit him—maybe Fyodor would know. He had experienced so much. *Yes,* Will thought, *Fyodor will have the answer.*

The spots of light that filtered through the trees were enough to wake everyone else as Will pondered. When he finally turned around, he saw that they had all begun to get ready. Liliu packed her pockets with what food there was while eating some leftover chicken. Fyodor was hunting a bug that had flown in through the open door, and Spartacus was having his share of leftovers as well.

"Good morning," Liliu said just as Fyodor's tongue darted out of his mouth, caught the fly in midair, and then pulled it just as quickly back into his mouth.

"Sorry, but breakfast is much easier as a frog," he said with a swallow.

Will smiled and helped Liliu pack what little food there was. Once they were finished, Will double-checked his pocket to make sure that the crystal was there; then he picked up the small potion bottle and, after ensuring that the lid was secure, placed it in his other pocket.

"Fyodor," Will said, starting to get a bit antsy about his gift, "I made something for you last night to thank you for giving me your sword."

"That's very kind of you, William, but you didn't have to."

"I know," Will told him, and then he reached under the cushion of his chair and pulled out a small but beautifully crafted version of a sword much like the one Fyodor had given him, complete with a small leather sheath that Will had trimmed from the excess material of the belt that was given to him.

Fyodor's large frog jaw dropped. With watery eyes, he leaped up onto the dresser and walked to the edge, where he received his new sword. "It is magnificent!"

Will had to smile. As proud of it as he was, it was just a filed-down and sharpened knitting needle, with a handle wrapped in blue cloth.

Fyodor pulled the blade from its leather sheath with a jerk and then held it triumphantly in the air, bringing it down slowly to a ready stance. With a few swift slices and jabs, he tested the blade's weight and then slid it back into its sheath. "Really, William, it is quite excellent. How did you learn such craftsmanship?"

"My father is a blacksmith," Will replied. "He's taught me a lot about swords."

"Your father is a wonderful teacher, and you both have my thanks."

"You're welcome," Will said, and then he turned to the door and let out a deep breath. "Now it's time to continue."

"That it is!" Fyodor declared as he tied the sword to his waist and leaped to the ground. "Come, and let the Darkness fear our approach!"

With all the confidence in the world, Fyodor marched out the door, and Will and Liliu shared a smile. Will could never have imagined Fyodor as defeated if he had not seen it with his own eyes. It was good to have him along.

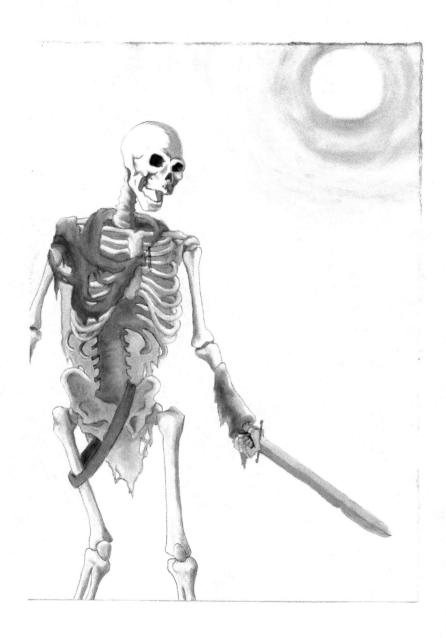

NINE

DEATH BASIN

T he Darkness thundered with fury. It had been defeated yet again, and this time by a girl. But now, it vowed, never again would it fail. It was time to unleash its greatest assassin—Agamemnon. This was a creature forged in the underworld; it had the body and head of a man, with the exception of its skull, which turned into a crown of horns at the top. Its skin, which was leathery and gray, only showed on its face and arms, because its chest and legs were covered in black armor. However, the breastplate split open on its back, allowing its four great wings to flap freely: two bat wings and two raven wings, one pair inside of the other. But most terrifying was the weapon that it held: a double-bladed ax of the blackest steel, as tall as Agamemnon himself, with veins of red sapphire that ran through the entire weapon. This assassin would not fail. The Darkness would not allow it.

Exploding from the rolling clouds, Agamemnon flapped its bat wings and glided on its raven wings. However, it would not go to William, as the others had. It would instead have William come to it—in Mountain Shadow Forest.

◄O►

William felt better about continuing now that he was rested and dry, and it seemed that everyone else felt the same. Light conversation passed the time easily as they walked through the forest of pine trees on a mat of pine needles. Liliu told Fyodor about her life and about how she and Will had met. Not amazingly, every story she told seemed to remind Fyodor of one of his own stories. But Will enjoyed listening to Fyodor. He was a good storyteller, and listening was better than the alternative of a quiet walk. Then, softly, along with Fyodor's voice, Will began to hear the trickle of a small stream.

"I think I hear water," Will said, interrupting Fyodor. "Sorry," he added, to which Fyodor nodded, and the group quieted down for a second.

"Ah," Fyodor exclaimed, "that is the stream I was talking about. Come—we should fill our water sacks."

The four of them made their way to the small trickle of water running through a shallow creek. Spartacus was the first to reach it, and he began lapping up every drop he could scoop with his long tongue. Will made his way upstream of Spartacus, so as not to get any of his saliva in his drinking bag, and then squatted down and let the water flow into his bag.

"Get as much water as you can," Fyodor said, removing the sword that Will had made for him, and then he jumped feet first into the water, which was not even deep enough to cover his body. "We are headed into a desert of utter desolation."

Liliu and Will finished filling their water bags as full as they could make them, and then both of them watched Fyodor roll around in the water. After a couple of turns, he noticed them watching and stood back on his hind legs and said, "Being a frog comes with its disadvantages as well. It seems that my skin dries out very easily."

"Are you going to be all right in the desert?" Liliu asked.

"We shall see," Fyodor replied, lowering himself back into the water. "Hopefully so."

Will and Liliu let Fyodor soak in the stream as long as he needed before they started off once again. As they went farther north, it got noticeably warmer. The pine trees were growing farther apart, and their needles were drier. Soon they reached an area with only the skeletal remains of dry, broken trees at the edge of a giant, desiccated basin. There, all vegetation ceased, and in front of them was only a seemingly endless expanse of shattered clay.

"Lake Caspian," Fyodor said, "or, as it is now known, Death Basin."

"This was a lake?" Will asked, astonished, as he watched the hot air wave over the miles of broken clay.

"The largest lake in the kingdom," Fyodor answered, moving on across the dry earth, "until the witch wars of Salem Arcane."

"What happened?" Liliu asked as she and Will took their first steps onto the slowly declining basin wall.

"The witch army had retreated into Pinewood Forest."

"Where we just were?" Will said.

"That forest is a puny reminder of the vast forest region it used to be," Fyodor said. "No, the army was where the marsh is now. King Ramses II used a cavalry of dragons to destroy a small mountain that was holding the water of this great lake. For two weeks, those giant beasts tore at the mountain until it finally gave, and the water poured into Pinewood Forest. The witches tried to flee, but the water came too fast, and in one afternoon, King Ramses the Great ended a war that had lasted thirty years. But as a consequence, the lake turned into a desert, and Pinewood Forest became the marsh where we met."

"But there are still witches there," Liliu said.

"Yes," Fyodor confirmed, nodding, "the flooding didn't kill all of them. In fact, many survived and continue to hide out there, attacking unsuspecting travelers."

Knowing the history of the area made Will appreciate

it more. As they walked along the fragile clay surface that crunched with every step, Will let his mind wander back and imagined what it would have looked like to see an entire lake drain into a forest.

After only twenty minutes of walking in the basin, Will was starting to wish they had started earlier. The sun was not even at its zenith in the sky, and beads of sweat were starting to pour down his forehead and back. To make things worse, there wasn't a cloud in the sky, so the group was taking the full brunt of the sun. But as bad as it was for Will and Liliu, it was worse for Spartacus, who was covered in hair and panting heavily, and worse still for Fyodor. Will could tell that the frog was trying to be tough, but once he began to stumble in the heat, Will offered him his shoulder. Fyodor humbly accepted, taking the side that was momentarily shaded by his head.

Will and Liliu were trying to use the water sparingly, but it seemed as if their throats would parch the moment they swallowed. On top of that, Fyodor needed the occasional dousing of water so that his skin did not become too dry. And then there was Spartacus, who needed just as much water as Will and Liliu. Altogether, their water bags lasted for only a couple of hours. But there was no way to tell how much farther they had to go, because in the distance, all they could see was the illusion of a lake rippling in the burning heat.

"How big is this lake, Fyodor?" Will asked, breaking the long silence.

"Great, my friend. We have probably only just begun."

"We're never gonna make it," Liliu moaned, holding up her empty water bag. "We should turn back and find another way round."

"There is no other way," Fyodor said. "The surrounding regions are too dangerous. There are goblins and even giants. This is the safest route."

"It won't be safe if the sun kills us," Liliu snapped.

Will didn't like the way she was speaking to Fyodor, but she had a point. "Fyodor, maybe she's right. Maybe we should go back and find a way around."

"No," Fyodor said decisively, "we must continue on. Bravery is not always about fighting what is on the outside. It is also about fighting your own discomfort and pushing on. So we shall continue."

Will and Liliu exchanged worried looks. Will wasn't so much concerned for himself or Liliu or even Fyodor; he was mainly worried about Spartacus. No matter where the sun moved in the sky, William made sure that Spartacus was in his shadow. Soon they were all struggling to keep walking. Will and Liliu were trudging slowly, and Spartacus was right by their side. Then, without warning, Fyodor fell from Will's shoulder. Luckily, Will reacted quickly and caught him before he hit the ground.

"Fyodor!" Will called out, but the frog didn't move.

"Is he okay?" Liliu asked, reaching out to him.

Will looked closely and noticed that he was still breathing, but who knew how much longer he would last in this heat? "We have to hurry," Will said, and he wrapped the frog in his shirt, which was wet with his sweat.

"Will, look," Liliu said, tapping him frantically on the shoulder. "It's a town."

Will had to rub his eyes to make sure he wasn't seeing an illusion, but sure enough, it was there—a small town raised above the basin floor. "It must have been an island."

"Yeah," Liliu agreed. "Come on—let's go."

Liliu started for it, and Will fell in behind her—one last push through the heat. But the closer they got to it, the worse the town looked. The buildings seemed old and deserted. They were all a grayish hue and looked to be in horrible condition. It was clear that the place was a ghost town, probably deserted when the lake was drained.

"Do you think there'll be water?" Liliu asked a bit hopelessly.

"I don't know, but it's worth looking, and if not, at least there'll be shade."

As they got closer, Will could see that it was some sort of harbor town. The dried and splintered wood of what was left of long docks stretched out from the island and into the desert.

The two of them reached the island's base and started the assent up its bank. Slowly, the buildings started to reveal themselves little by little. The paint of the town had been burned off long ago, leaving only the desiccated wood that was riddled with cracks.

The last few feet of the bank were steep enough that Will had to give Fyodor to Liliu and climb up on his hands and knees. Then he turned back to Liliu and helped pull her and Spartacus to the top. After Liliu returned Fyodor to Will, the two of them turned toward the town. It was more obvious now than ever that it was deserted. They made their way to the end of a long, empty street that disappeared into the island. There was no doubt that this was once a thriving city, but now only empty buildings were left.

"Where should we start?" Liliu asked.

"It would take forever to go from building to building."

"We have to start somewhere," Liliu said. "I'll take the right side of the street, and you take the left?"

Will nodded reluctantly and then turned to Spartacus. "Go with Liliu." The exhausted Spartacus looked up at Will and then headed over to Liliu.

"Are you looking out for me?" Liliu said sarcastically.

"Nope, Spartacus is," Will responded smoothly, and then he started toward the first building on the left. A wooden boardwalk ran in front of the buildings for the length of the block and then turned a sharp corner. Cautiously, Will stepped onto the first beams, slowly shifting his weight. The boards cracked under his foot but managed to hold, so Will stepped up onto the platform and then continued slowly to the first door. It was already ajar, so Will gave it a light push, and it swung open to reveal a welcoming cool. Inside, the wood was preserved much better; even the paint, while faded, was still in place. But before stepping in, Will looked back and saw Spartacus disappear into the building across the street.

Will stepped into what was obviously some kind of store. It had shelves, which were all barren, and a few glass cases that had been broken into. Will realized that he wasn't the first person to come back through this town since it was deserted. *Who knows how many people have come through here looking for water?* Will thought. Regardless, he couldn't give up. Fyodor needed him. Will looked down at his new companion, who was still wrapped up in his shirt. He didn't seem any worse, but Will hated seeing such a lively creature unconscious.

Will was just about to give up on this vacant shop, when something caught his eye. Looking closer, he realized there was a boot lying behind one of the counters. The way it was resting, back on its heel, made Will want to investigate. Cautiously, Will approached it, but each step was accompanied by cracks and whines of the wood beneath his feet. He didn't know why he bothered moving slowly, but somehow, a fast approach didn't seem right.

As Will got closer, more of the boot revealed itself until he saw a second boot and then trousers, which led to a tattered brown shirt and then to the shriveled remains of a man's neck and head. There was no telling how long the body had been there, but all that was left were the skin and the bone. Grossly captivated by the sight, Will noticed that its arms were folded back underneath its body, and that was when he noticed the strap that cut across its chest. *Maybe it was a water bag?* Chances were that it was empty, but Will decided it was worth a look, even if he had to touch the remains.

Carefully, Will stepped over the body, bent down, and took the strap between two fingers. Then he began to pull it around the corpse, which caused it to start twisting awkwardly. Will tried to adjust the strap so that the desecrated body wouldn't move with it, but it was no use—wherever the strap went, the body followed. Cringing, Will grabbed the strap tightly and then, in one swift motion, yanked upward. The fragile body nearly fell to pieces, but the remaining skin managed to hold the brittle bones together as it twisted sharply to its side. Sure enough, beneath the corpse, a water sack was connected to the strap.

Will, deciding that he didn't want to tangle with the skeleton anymore, set Fyodor gently on the counter, drew his sword, and slid the blade under the strap. With a swift motion, he cut the strap and then pulled the bag free. Next, he took Fyodor back into his hands and turned to leave, when Liliu stepped in the door, sending Will almost to the ceiling.

"Did I scare you?" Liliu said with a smirk. "Sorry."

"That's okay," Will replied, trying to recover his composure.

"What did you find?"

"A skeleton," Will said, and then he held up the water bag. "And maybe some water."

"There was a skeleton in the other place too. That's what I came in here to tell you," Liliu said. Then she looked at the water bag. "Is there water in it?"

"It feels like there could be, but not much," Will said. He handed Fyodor to Liliu and pulled the top off the water bag. Slowly, he started to tip the bag over Fyodor, but nothing came out. Finally, when the bag was almost completely upside down, a trickle of water poured from the lip onto Fyodor's face. It seemed to be just enough to revive him. Slowly, his eyes opened.

"Did we make it?" Fyodor asked groggily.

"No," Will answered, "not yet; we're at an abandoned island."

"Iliad Island," Fyodor rasped, and his consciousness began to fade again. "A well ... middle of town ... after draining."

"A well?" Liliu repeated.

"Yes," Fyodor confirmed, and then he slipped back into unconsciousness.

Will and Liliu looked at each other, and neither of them had to say a thing. A moment later, they were both out the door and headed to the middle of town. After a couple of sharp turns past more rows of decrepit buildings and only a short bit of searching, they made it to the town square in the center of the island. In the middle of the square was the circular stone structure of a well. As fast as they could in their poor condition, they rushed toward it, and as soon as Will reached it, he looked down into a deep blackness. Liliu, meanwhile, began looking around for a stone, which she quickly found and dropped into the abyss. The sharp clash of stone on stone echoed up the well until it ended with the unmistakable sound of splashing water. Will and Liliu were so excited by the sound that they hugged each other, almost squishing Fyodor between them. But they soon came to their senses and backed away. Will wasn't sure, but he felt as if he were blushing as much as Liliu.

"We need a rope," Will said quickly so that they could look somewhere else besides at each other.

"Right," Liliu agreed, and they both began looking around.

Spartacus soon joined in, sniffing near the well, although Will was sure he didn't know what he was looking for.

"Over here!" Liliu yelled, and Will ran to her side. She had found a length of rope on the back of the carcass of what had once been a horse. As quickly as possible, she plucked it from the remains and shook the dust off it. "Why are there so many skeletons around?"

"Maybe they all came here looking for water?" Will said, taking an end of the rope and tying his water bag to it.

"But there's a well right there," Liliu countered. Will just shrugged. He was thirsty, and right now, he didn't care; he just wanted to get water.

After the water bag was secure, he and Liliu lowered it slowly into the well. Luckily, there was just enough rope to allow the bag to touch the water if Will leaned deep into in the well while holding Liliu's hand for support. His bag filled surprisingly quickly, allowing him to move on to Liliu's bag. Soon both water bags were full, and the four of them, including an unconscious Fyodor, retreated into the shade of one of the town-square shops. Will placed Fyodor on a table, and Liliu began pouring the cool well water over him. In seconds, Fyodor was sputtering and coughing while rolling around in the pool of water that had formed on the tabletop.

"Ahhh," Fyodor declared as he sat up, glistening once again. "Just what I needed. Thank you, both of you."

Will and Liliu smiled. They were happy to see their friend awake again, and now it was their turn. First, Will poured a stream in front of Spartacus, who was quick to lap up as much as he could. When Will stopped pouring, the dog started licking the wet floor. Then Will and Liliu chugged as much as they could until the bottles were empty once again.

"Where did you find the water?" Fyodor asked when they had finished hydrating themselves.

"In the well that you told us about," Liliu answered, a bit confused.

"Oh, very good," Fyodor said. "To be honest, I thought it would be dry."

Everyone laughed at their good fortune. Then they all took seats at the table that Fyodor was sitting on, and Liliu pulled out a bit of food, which they all shared.

"We should wait until dusk to start again," Fyodor said. "I think it will be wiser to travel in the cool of night rather than in the heat of day."

Will wasn't going to argue, and it seemed that Liliu wasn't either. So they stayed in the shop for the rest of the day, only going out once to get more water. But the heat and dehydration had taken their toll on the group, and they all ended up falling asleep in the cool shop. Even Fyodor, whom Will could tell was trying to stay awake, struggled with his own exhaustion and eventually gave in.

William opened his eyes to the dim fiery-orange hues of late dusk. Lazily, he rubbed his fingers in his eyes and looked around at Liliu and Fyodor. Liliu was still fast asleep with her arms folded and her head down on the table, and Fyodor was curled up beside her, sleeping soundly as well. He glanced down and saw Spartacus raise his eyebrows; apparently, he was waiting for them to wake up. Will took a sip of water from his water bag and was about to reach down to give some to Spartacus, when he heard footsteps outside on the boardwalk. The steps started softly, but the whine of the boards and the thud of the boots on the old wood were growing. Someone was approaching. A low growl rolled from Spartacus's throat as Will slowly brought his hand to the hilt of the sword. But just as the steps reached the door, they disappeared.

Will's first instinct told him that someone was waiting for him on the other side of the wall. Maybe he'd heard Will and had frozen? Cautiously, Will stood and began making his way around the door in a way that would reveal the stranger while keeping him at a safe distance. But when he got to the point where he could see outside, he saw nothing.

"What are you doing?" Liliu asked groggily. Her voice made Will jump once again.

"I heard footsteps outside."

"Footsteps?" Fyodor repeated. He had obviously just woken up as well.

"Yeah," Will said. "They stopped right outside the door, but now nobody's there."

"Are you sure that you weren't dreaming?" Liliu asked.

"Yes," Will shot back.

Fyodor stood, quickly stretched, and then said, "It's time to go. Do we have enough water?"

"I need more," Liliu said, holding up her water bag. "It's almost empty."

"Come then," Fyodor said, and he leaped off the table to the floor. "We need to move quickly."

"Is something wrong?" Will asked.

"I have a feeling that this place is going to become very unwelcoming very quickly," Fyodor answered as he started out the door.

The others followed and made their way to the well, where they tied Liliu's bag to the rope and lowered it down. As they waited in silence for it to fill, it became apparent that Will hadn't been hearing things. All over the wood walkways, footsteps were thumping, and some were even crunching through the dirt by the well. Spartacus's head was shifting at every sound, but nobody could be seen in the failing light. Then doors started to open and close in many of the buildings, and an occasional voice would find their ears.

"Is it full yet?" Will whispered urgently as his eyes bounced from one empty doorway to the next.

"It's close enough," Liliu answered, and she began pulling up the bottle as quickly as she could. Meanwhile, more footsteps were drumming across the boardwalks all around them with no one to claim them. Finally, the water bag was in her hand, and she yanked it free from the rope, almost tearing the cap off. As quickly as possible, she threw the strap around her, and they started toward one of the open streets. After only a few steps, the sun disappeared below the horizon, and all was revealed.

Will, Liliu, Fyodor, and Spartacus froze in place. Standing ominously on the boardwalk that surrounded them were transparent pale-blue ghosts. Their faces showed expressions of animosity. It was clear that Will and his friends were not welcome. In the tense silence, Will waited for Fyodor to say something, but apparently, he was as stunned as the rest of them. Even Spartacus was quiet, meekly hiding between Will and the well. Suddenly, one of the ghosts let out a terrible cry and charged. Will stumbled over Spartacus as he tried to retreat, causing Liliu to back into him. This created a clumsy withdrawal, which wasn't fast enough to avoid the charge.

The malevolent ghost was almost on them. As Will raised his hand to his face, he saw Fyodor leap into the air and slice his sword along the ghost's face, but the blade went right through, as if he were cutting into water. Then the ghost reached out for Will with long, grotesque fingers, but when they touched his throat, they passed right through him like a cold wind. With a shiver, the entire phantom passed through his body. Will snapped around and saw it continue back to the other side of the square, where it rejoined the other pale-blue ghosts.

"Are you okay?" Liliu asked frantically.

"I think so," Will replied, a bit unsure if he was or not.

"Come," Fyodor ordered. "We must go through the ghosts."

"Through the ghosts!" Liliu spat. "Are you crazy?"

"They can't hurt us," Fyodor said, trying to comfort

her, but she was still hesitant, and meanwhile, another ghost charged. It came screaming at them with all the fury it could muster. In a flash, Liliu pulled out her slingshot and snapped a stone at the ghost, but the projectile flew right through it, just as the ghost itself passed through her.

"Liliu!" Will couldn't help but call out, even though he knew she was okay.

"I'm all right," she said a bit distantly. Then she looked at Fyodor. "Let's make a run for it."

Fyodor nodded, but just as he did, the ghosts started to move all at once. With their eyes locked on Will and his companions, they started to drift away back into the town; some floated down streets, while others disappeared into buildings.

"Now!" Fyodor yelled. "Let's move!"

The four of them exploded into a sprint, and Liliu snatched Fyodor off the ground. They darted through the deserted town square to one of the main streets, which would take them out of town, but the moment they started down the long dirt road, they froze in their tracks. Will nearly ran into Liliu but managed to swing his body to the side while still staring straight ahead. A skeleton, softly glowing in the pale moonlight and still dressed in the ratty clothes it had been wearing at its death, stepped menacingly from the boardwalk and turned to face them.

Without having to say a word, the four of them doubled back at once. Fyodor leaped into Will's hands, and they raced around a corner and sprinted down another long dirt road that they hoped would lead them out of the haunted town. But in the distance, more ghouls emerged from the building, walking awkwardly into the street. Some were armed with swords or planks of wood, while others had only their bony fingers to attack with, but all of them were focused on Will and his friends.

"They're everywhere!" Liliu cried.

"Fyodor, what should we do?" Will asked, hoping the frog would have some clever plan to get them out of this situation.

"We fight," Fyodor said, and he leaped from Will's hand.

In a flash, Will drew the sword that Fyodor had given him and held it ready. He was no swordsman, but working as a blacksmith with his father had given him a certain understanding when it came to blades. Meanwhile, Liliu began looking around for stones. Luckily, good-sized rocks were scattered everywhere, so she quickly gathered a few and placed one of them in the slingshot, ready to go. Spartacus was as fierce as ever, with the hair on his neck standing straight up and his teeth showing with a tremendous growl. They were ready, and they started down the road with their backs to each other so that they could watch all directions. Unfortunately, the skeletons seemed unimpressed and continued to close in.

As slow as the ghouls were, their unrelenting approach and ominous, eyeless gazes were unnerving. Will found that his courage was starting to slip. He wanted to run for it— right through them as fast as he could—and hope everything would be all right. *But now is not the time for hope,* Will thought. *Now is the time for action.* With a deep breath, Will tightened his grip on his sword.

The first ghoul lunged clumsily at Liliu. It was unarmed, with bony fingers outstretched. Liliu snapped her slingshot, and a stone crashed into the ghoul's head, shattering the top of its skull. Staggering backward for only a moment, the ghoul quickly regained its composure and continued the charge. Liliu started to reload, but the monster was almost on her, so without thinking, Will slashed downward with his sword. He was amazed at how easily it cut through the undead bones of the skeleton's arms. The ghoul let out a hissing shriek and stumbled back, but it quickly collected itself and then lunged again with its broken limbs outstretched. Liliu snapped another stone, and the rest of the ghoul's skull exploded as Will hacked across its bony body, cutting easily through its ribs. The skeleton crumbled to the ground, where a blue mist raised from its remains in the steamy figure of a man, and then drifted off into the buildings.

"They're the ghosts!" Will called out before turning to the next skeleton.

"And they can be defeated!" Fyodor declared as one of the undead swung an ax at the frog's head. Fyodor was too fast for the brittle creature. He ducked the blade and leaped onto the ghoul's shoulders. This caught the attention of another skeleton, which began hacking wildly at Fyodor, who, in a display of amazing agility, began flipping and tumbling between the two ghouls, causing them to shatter each other's bones with their own clumsy strikes.

Meanwhile, Liliu shot stone after stone at the approaching skeletons while Will used Fyodor's sword to slash through them like butter. Even Spartacus joined in the fight, biting the legs of the skeletons and then running off with their limbs, leaving them helplessly crawling on the ground.

Pieces of bone flew all around Will as he hacked through the ghosts, until suddenly, his sword clanged with another. He had met a ghoul with a weapon. It pushed Will's blade away and swung, but Will jumped back, and the tip of the sword zipped across Will's shirt. The skeleton swung again, and again, Will was forced to retreat.

"William!" Fyodor yelled as he bounced from undead to undead. "Defend and counter! Backing away only gives him power."

Without allowing his mind to argue, Will raised his sword, and he heard the ring and felt the jerk as the attacker's blade hit his own.

"Now, William!" Fyodor screamed. "Strike back!"

But Will had waited too long, and the ghoul struck again. More out of reflex than skill, Will managed to block, but this time, he attacked back. With a whirl of his blade, he cut across the skeleton's neck, and its head rolled backward and fell to the ground. But to Will's surprise, the skeleton was not finished and swung again. Will barely managed to duck. He could feel the air blow past his hair as the blade swept by and then rounded and came back toward his head. Without thinking, he brought his sword up and, with a clang, managed another block. Then, in a blur of anger and fear, Will struck back with a slash that cut through the skeleton's torso. Its brittle ribs shattered to pieces in the wake of the sword, and the undead creature crumbled to the ground.

"Good work, William!" Fyodor shouted as he jumped from a recently defeated undead corpse. "Liliu, Spartacus, let's go!"

With one final rock, Liliu knocked an undead to the ground with a shot to the face, and Spartacus darted past a skeleton, knocking it to the ground. William fell in behind them, bending down as he passed Fyodor so that the frog could jump onto his back, and then the four of them raced down the road. Skeletons that got in their way were cut down by Will or knocked down by Liliu with a well-placed stone. Soon they reached the island's edge, and with an army of undead behind them, they jumped back into the basin, sliding on their backsides down the hill to the dry clay below.

Once at the bottom, they looked up and, in the bright moonlight, saw a line of skeletons at the island's edge, all looking malevolently down at William and his companions. But it was clear that none of the ghosts were going to pursue the group further. While keeping an eye on them, Will and his companions retreated northward. Even when they got to a point where they could no longer see the island, they glanced back every few seconds just to be sure that none had followed them.

TEN

FAIRIES AND PIXIES

Exhausted and cold, William finally took his first few steps from Death Basin. Spartacus was at his heels, and Liliu and Fyodor were just beside him. Past the horizon, the distant glow of the sun had just begun to arrive, and now once again, Will was happy to welcome its warmth.

"Why is it always coldest just before the sun rises?" Will groaned. It was a rhetorical question that received an "I don't know" mumbled from Liliu; however, Fyodor had an answer.

"So that we may appreciate the warmth more when it touches us."

Will glanced down at his new friend and knew that he was right, but it didn't make the cold any easier. He was starting to wish he had retrieved his coat from the witches.

"Where are we?" Liliu asked, and Will remembered he had left the map with the witches as well.

"We are near Mountain Shadow Forest," Fyodor answered, and then he pointed ahead to the hills that were just becoming visible in the dawn light. "It's just over those hills, a journey of a couple of hours."

Will started to feel his muscles whine at the mention of a couple more hours of walking. "I need to take a break," he said, and out of the corner of his eye, he saw Liliu nodding.

"Me too. I'm exhausted," she agreed.

"It has been a long day and night," Fyodor said understandingly. "You should be proud of all that you have done. We deserve a rest."

Will didn't waste a second; he plopped down onto the soft patch of grass beneath his feet. A moment later, Liliu collapsed next to him, followed shortly by Spartacus after he circled a few times. Fyodor, on the other hand, crouched on all fours gracefully and began scanning the air for a meal. Liliu pulled a few handfuls of nuts and berries from her pocket, which she had taken from Fyodor's cabin, and shared them with Will and Spartacus. Still cold but otherwise content, Will shoveled them into his mouth. He had just begun to chew noisily, when he felt the ground under him shake slightly.

"What was that?" Liliu asked before Will could.

Will was about to shrug, when he saw Fyodor and Spartacus spring to their feet simultaneously. In an instant, they were both fully alert. The ground shook again, but this time, a distant drumming accompanied the movement, as though something large were beating the earth.

"A giant," Fyodor said urgently, and Will and Liliu jumped back to their feet.

"Should we run back into the desert?" Liliu asked desperately, staring back into Death Basin.

"No," Fyodor answered. "We need to find a place to hide."

But it was too late. In the distance, under the glow of the sun, a huge creature built like a man, with pale skin and half a tree in his right hand, was running awkwardly toward them. Its immense legs were trying to move as fast as possible, but their sheer girth was causing it to stumble awkwardly over the hilly terrain.

"This way!" Liliu cried, and she began sprinting as fast as she could toward the distant forest. Will scooped up Fyodor and then chased after her with Spartacus at his heels.

"We cannot outrun it!" Fyodor yelled as the thundering footsteps of the approaching giant grew behind them. "We must find a place to hide!"

Will couldn't help but look back. The enormous beast was gaining, even with its clumsy stride. Frantically, he began scanning the area around them, but there were only rolling hills, without so much as a tree to hide behind. Then he heard Liliu.

"There!" she screamed, and she cut to her right. Will quickly followed and immediately saw what she saw. A cave, just big enough for the four of them, was a short distance ahead. Will could feel the ground tremble with every footstep that the great creature took. Unable to help himself, he looked back again, and to his amazement, it was right on them. With a roar, it raised its giant club and brought it crashing back down. Unable to think, Will dived to his right, and the tree smashed into the ground behind him. Fyodor had to leap from Will's hand to avoid being crushed. With great agility, the frog rolled to his feet and drew his small sword. But they were no match for the giant, and Will knew it.

"Go!" Will yelled. It was clear that the giant wanted him, and as long as it focused on him, the others could get to safety. But they wouldn't abandon him. Liliu swooped up a rock as Fyodor took a great leap onto the huge monster. Spartacus darted around its legs, barking and snarling. As fast as he could, Will leaped to his feet, but he had to immediately dive again to avoid being crushed by another blow. Pebbles and dirt showered around him. Will jumped up again, looking for the next blow, but the giant had paused and begun swatting at its own face. Fyodor had climbed to its head and was slashing at the creature's eyes. Unfortunately, Fyodor couldn't fight against the giant's huge hands and was forced to quickly retreat. He leaped from the giant's shoulders and landed perfectly on Spartacus, who darted for the caves.

Just as the giant regained its composure, a stone from Liliu's slingshot struck it in the nose. The beast let out a roar and erupted into a tantrum, slamming its club into the ground around it. The distraction was enough for Liliu and Will to sprint to the cave.

Once inside, the group began backing quickly away from the entrance. Dirt lightly showered down around them as the giant thundered outside. Then an eerie silence settled—but only for a moment, as the creature's huge head suddenly appeared in the entrance, with its large, beady eyes searching frantically. For a second, they locked on Will, and then the giant forced a large, pale arm into the opening and began clutching desperately at the air. What little light there was disappeared as the giant pressed its body tighter against the entrance. In the darkness, Will could feel the wind of the giant's hand grabbing frantically at the air, hoping to seize them, but they were just out of reach. Even so, Will continued to back up, using the wall to guide him until he bumped into Liliu.

"Sorry," he apologized, and he heard Spartacus whine. Will knew Spartacus didn't like the dark any more than the rest of them did.

"How far do you think the cave goes?" Liliu asked.

"This is not a cave," Fyodor said. "It's the burrow of a Phoenician mole rat, a large but harmless creature. However, their burrows can go on for miles."

"Do you think it will come out somewhere else?" Will asked, turning himself cautiously so that he didn't accidently step on Fyodor.

"It's likely," Fyodor replied, and then a beam of light caught Fyodor's figure, followed by a sprinkle of pebbles and dirt.

Will glanced back at the opening—the giant was gone, but the thundering was back, and it was louder this time. "He's trying to cause a cave-in," Will yelled, and the four of them hurried deeper into the cave as large clumps of dirt and rock started to fall behind them. Moments later, the entrance was completely destroyed. The cave was pitch black once again. William couldn't see his hand in front of his face, and he was waving it right in front of his nose.

"What do we do now?" he heard Liliu say from somewhere in front of him.

"William," Fyodor called out, "unsheathe your sword."

Without thinking twice, Will pulled the sword from its sheath, and as he did, a soft white light poured into the cave around them. The blade was glowing.

"A light," Fyodor said, "courtesy of Voltaire. He enchanted my blade with a spell that allows it to glow when all sunlight has vanished."

Will and Liliu gazed at the sword in awe. As much light as it gave off, it was not too bright to look at; rather, it looked as though a light were shining on it.

"It looks like the moon," Liliu said, and Will nodded.

"Come along now, my friends," Fyodor said as a few more clumps of dirt fell behind them. "We need to get moving."

With Will in the lead, the four of them navigated forward. To Will's amazement, the tunnel soon forked into many tunnels, which forked into more tunnels. They had wandered into a maze. At one point, they came to a tunnel that was under construction. One of the huge Phoenician mole rats was nonchalantly digging a new hole. It took little notice of Will and the others as it chewed through dirt and stone.

"We're gonna get lost down here," Liliu said as they made another turn down another tunnel. "Fyodor, do you have any idea where we're going?"

"Yes," Fyodor said a little impatiently, and then he pointed forward down the long, dark tunnel. "That way."

"Thanks," Liliu said sarcastically. "I feel much better now."

Will had to smile. He was starting to learn that he could always count on Liliu to lighten the mood. As their journey continued, the unchanging scenery of the caves made it seem as if they never made any progress. Will was about to protest their direction, when a tiny light glimmered in the distance.

"Sheath the sword," Fyodor ordered. "Quickly."

Will slid the blade into the sheath as fast as he could, but the light in the distance remained.

"We've made it!" Liliu exclaimed, but Fyodor hushed her.

"That is not the sun," Fyodor said, and just as he said that, the light began to move on its own. In the darkness, Will could hear the small metallic glide of Fyodor drawing his sword. Then, suddenly, more lights sparkled and glowed in the distance. They were approaching.

"William," Fyodor whispered, "when I say to do so, draw your sword."

Will foolishly nodded in the dark but quickly caught himself and whispered back, "Okay."

The tiny golden specks of light bounced along in the darkness, but as they approached, they didn't seem to get much bigger. In fact, they were quite small, like bounding golden stars. Just before they came close enough for their light to illuminate Will and his friends, Fyodor whispered intensely, "Now!"

Will yanked the blade free, and light poured around them and onto the glowing creatures. The beings quickly pulled their own tiny arms and then froze, just as Fyodor had.

"Fairies," William said aloud without meaning to. He had heard many stories about them and had always wanted to see one, and now they were flying right in front of him and were everything he had imagined them to be. They were about four inches tall and glowed with a golden light not unlike his sword, which gave off light without being bright. They all had bright blue eyes, pointy ears, and four small transparent wings that buzzed furiously behind them. Amazingly, they were wearing armor—bright golden armor with intricate, swirling designs on every piece.

"Who are you?" one of the fairies asked confidently, looking directly at William.

"We are travelers," Fyodor answered with his sword still ready. "And who are you?"

"I am Vespasian," the tallest of the three fairies said, and then he gestured to his right and left as he introduced his compatriots. "And this is Domitian and Constantine. Now, please, grant us the courtesy of introducing yourselves."

Impressed with their manners, William began to introduce himself, but Fyodor quickly interrupted. "With all due respect, we wish to keep our business our own."

"I see," Vespasian replied. "It is wise of you to do so, but your secrecy reveals everything. However, fear not, for we are on your side."

"Then can you point us the way out?" Fyodor asked as he sheathed his sword. William almost did the same but quickly caught himself.

"I would be happy to, but you must know that you're in great danger," Vespasian said, looking directly at William.

"Tell us something that we don't know," Liliu said sarcastically.

"You are aware of the pixies then?" Vespasian asked.

"What pixies?" Fyodor shot back, returning their attention to him.

"The witches—they have sent an army after him," Vespasian replied, pointing at William.

"Of pixies?" Liliu said incredulously.

"Yes," Vespasian answered.

"During the witch wars," Fyodor explained, "a fairy civil war erupted when many of the fairies joined the witches. Those that did were labeled as pixies, or traitors, in fairy language."

Vespasian nodded and then said, "And since your escape, a call for your head has been made."

Just then, a golden light, buzzing furiously, zipped down the tunnel and stopped in front of Vespasian, panting for air.

"Vespasian," the fairy panted, "the western ... entrance ... has been sealed."

"That's all but one," Domitian declared.

"It's a trap," Constantine said quietly to Vespasian but loudly enough for Will to hear.

"Perhaps, but we have no other choice," Vespasian said, and then he turned to the fairy that had just arrived still panting for air. "Do you have strength enough to summon the others?"

"I do," the fairy said, snapping to attention, "and I will."

"Very good, Pertinax. Then may fortune be with you," Vespasian said, and Pertinax darted away, leaving a trail of golden dust behind him. "Come," Vespasian continued. "We have no time to waste. There is one more way out of these caves, and we must get there before it is sealed shut."

"Who is sealing them?" William asked as Fyodor leaped onto his shoulder.

"Agents of the Darkness," Vespasian said as William and the others fell in behind him.

"How did they know we were in here?" Liliu asked.

"A pixie probably saw you enter and spread the information," Vespasian said, and then he looked back at Will as he continued to fly. "The Darkness knows that with you trapped down here, you will not be able to stop it."

Suddenly, the idea that he really was the one started to sink into Will's mind, and that seemed to scare him more than anything he had yet faced. The idea that everything rested in his hands was more than he wanted to think about. So he shook the thought from his mind and focused on where he was.

"Thank you for your aid, Vespasian," Fyodor said. "We owe you an introduction."

"Your courtesy is appreciated, but it can wait for now," Vespasian said as he led the group down one tunnel after another.

To Will, it seemed as though they were making a turn every hundred feet. At one point, Will and Liliu exchanged concerned looks; they were completely trusting that Vespasian knew where he was going.

"This place is a labyrinth," Liliu remarked.

"That it is," Vespasian replied. "But these tunnels have been a hideout for fairies for many decades. We know them well."

More turns and more tunnels of dirt stretched in front of them. Then, slowly, the dirt began to turn to a rough gravel and finally to solid stone.

"We have reached the Fujiwara Caves," Vespasian said. Will watched him pull a small diamond-blue blade from his sheath, and they all slowed. "We are not far from the cave opening now."

As they crept slowly across the stone floor, William's sword light started to vanish into a void of darkness. They were obviously entering a large area—so large, in fact, that it had a breeze that washed gently against William's face.

"The exit is close," Vespasian whispered, and they continued to creep slower than ever.

"Why don't we make a run for it?" Liliu whispered back.

"I'm sure there is a trap somewhere, waiting for us," Vespasian answered softly, and just then, a soft red glow began to grow at the far end of the huge cave. With their eyes locked forward, the group slowly came to a halt as one dot of bloodred light at a time floated into the distant darkness. Soon an entire swarm had gathered. In an incredible display of order, the dots organized themselves into perfect fiery-red columns, five high and many more deep.

"A pixie army," Fyodor said, and Vespasian nodded silently.

Will's first thought was to sheath his sword, but it was too late—they knew he was there, and they were going to attack.

"There are so many," Liliu said absentmindedly as the three fairies aligned themselves into a triangular formation.

"What are we going to do?" Will asked.

"We will run—right through them," Vespasian said, and Will, Liliu, Fyodor, and even Spartacus looked at him.

"Are you crazy?" Liliu interjected. "They'll cut us to pieces!"

"We have no other option," Vespasian said adamantly, and Domitian and Constantine drew their swords. "If we run, they'll chase us."

"Attack it is," Fyodor said, drawing his sword once again as he looked up at Vespasian from the ground. "I am Fyodor, she is Liliu, the valiant dog is Spartacus, and our young hero is William." Everyone nodded as he or she was introduced. "We thank you for your courage."

Vespasian nodded back, and then he pointed his sword toward the glowing pixie army and took a deep breath. Will could feel his stomach tighten and his heart pound. If a charge was what they were going to do, then he would do it. With gritted teeth, William prepared himself to break into a sprint, when suddenly, a soft golden glow, followed by the echoing buzz of hundreds of wings, emerged behind him. Everyone spun around just in time to see the fairy army appear. The fairies were all decorated in golden armor as detailed as Vespasian's, and as they swarmed into the cavern, they drew their own diamond-blue swords. In front of William and his friends, they formed into golden rows and columns just as the pixies had done.

"Your army, sir," Pertinax said, still panting.

"Well done, Pertinax," Vespasian said proudly. "Now,

join the formation at the rear, and find your breath in the next few moments."

"Yes, sir," the fairy said, and then he darted off to join the others.

William watched Vespasian look on proudly at his compatriots. Then, once they all fell into position, he yelled with a tremendous voice, "To arms, my brothers and sisters! Today we remember that darkness can never fall in the light, and we are the light!"

William could feel his hopes begin to rise, and he could tell that Liliu was feeling the same way. She was scanning the ground for rocks, and fortunately, there were plenty. Soon she had a handful, with one loaded in her slingshot.

"William!" Vespasian hollered over the sound of the fairies' beating wings. "Stay behind us. We will be your shield."

William nodded. He wanted to say something heroic, but nothing came to mind, so he just brought the tip of his sword to the ready. Meanwhile, Fyodor had made his way under the fairies' formation toward the front. Will knew that Fyodor wasn't going to miss the battle. Liliu and Spartacus flanked him to his right and left.

At the far end of the cavern, the red lights began to flicker as the pixies pumped their wings, causing a dull roar to echo through the darkness. In reply, the fairies did the same, and soon the entire cavern was engulfed in the buzzing thunder of thousands of wings.

Vespasian made his way to the front of the formation and again pointed his sword toward the pixies, but this time, he yelled, "Charge!"

The two armies, one red and one gold, flew furiously toward each other, their collective wings roaring. On Will's right, Liliu had a stone ready in her slingshot, and she was bobbing it up and down, looking for a shot, but she couldn't take it without possibly hitting one of the fairies. Then, in an explosion of color, the two armies collided with the ring of a thousand bells. Immediately, fairies and pixies began to fall to the ground, their lights flickering out as they dropped.

A number of pixies were darting back and forth, obviously trying to get around the fairy lines so that they could get to William, but the fairies were matching their movements. All the while, Fyodor was leaping into the air, slashing at the pixies. Some of them were able to defend themselves, but most could not, and they fell lifelessly to the stone floor. Liliu started to make her way around the fairy lines with her slingshot at the ready, but it seemed as if every time she had a clear shot, it quickly disappeared as fairies and pixies darted about. Then, finally, one of the pixies shot straight up and started to charge forward toward Will, but the moment it shot forward, it was struck with a stone that sent it somersaulting through the air.

"Nice shot," Will said as Liliu loaded another rock into her string.

"Thank you," she replied, scanning the air for more targets.

A number of pixies dropped stealthily below their formation and darted toward Will. Liliu immediately fired, but the swarm expanded, and the rock flew right through them, missing its target. All at once, they collapsed back into a tight formation. Fyodor leaped into the air and managed to cut one of them from the assault; however, four others were still charging. Liliu fired again. This time, she just managed to graze one of them. The pixie tumbled to the ground and bounced twice but somehow quickly managed to regain its composure. It was about to leap back into the air, when Spartacus snatched it with his powerful jaws.

Back at the front lines, a number of fairies broke formation and shot off after the pixies, but the pixies were closing fast. Will began swinging wildly, hoping to scare them off. Unfortunately, they were undeterred. With great agility, they maneuvered through his swings and cut past Will's body, each one slicing deep into his skin with its own red diamond sword. Will gritted his teeth as the blades slashed into him, and just when he thought they had passed, he felt his skin get pierced again from behind. They were swarming around him like bees. Spartacus started jumping into the air, snapping wildly, but they were too fast, zooming away from his teeth just in time. Meanwhile, Will could see Liliu looking for a shot, but he knew she couldn't take it without possibly hitting him.

"If you have a shot, take it!" Will called out.

"I don't want to hit you!" she objected, and instead, she ran to him and started swatting at his attackers with her hands. In response, one of the pixies broke away from Will and started to attack Liliu.

Finally, Fyodor arrived with a team of fairies. They immediately engaged the pixies, and a midair sword battle erupted around Will and Liliu. Fyodor was hopping all over, slashing and striking at the pixies, until one of the glowing red soldiers engaged Fyodor on the ground. Their small swords clashed and hummed in a dangerous dance.

More pixies broke away from the main battle and jetted toward Will, but this time, Liliu was ready for them. Ignoring what was happening around her, she raised her slingshot and fired. The stone hammered into the leading pixie, knocking it back against two others, but there were still three more coming. Liliu loaded again and raised the slingshot, but before she could fire, the string snapped. One of the pixies had cut it while flying by. Furious, Liliu threw the handle, which managed to strike one of the incoming soldiers and knock it to the cavern floor, where Spartacus finished it off.

Will felt helpless; all around Liliu and him, a battle was

raging as pixies and fairies fought ferociously. He wanted to engage with his own sword, but it was too large to be a threat to the quick and agile pixies. So he was forced to stand there and watch as Fyodor, with a quick thrust to the abdomen, finished the pixie that had engaged him, and then the frog wasted no time leaping back into the air again and again, attacking wherever he could.

As the battle wore on, the pixies were noticeably losing, which allowed more and more fairies to come to Will's aid and fight off any pixie soldiers that made it to him. Finally, the pixies began to retreat. Most of the fairies held their ground and watched them run, while others chased them to the cave exit. Soon all the pixies had fled, leaving only the golden auras of fairies buzzing about.

"William!" Vespasian called out as he raced over to him. "Are you all right?"

"A little scratched up, but I'm okay," Will said as he put pressure on his deepest wound, at the top of his shoulder.

"And, Liliu," Fyodor said as he sheathed his sword, "how are you?"

"About the same," Liliu replied.

After hearing that Liliu was all right, Will immediately began looking around for Spartacus. He quickly found him squatting a few feet away, licking his own wounds. Will went over to make sure he wasn't cut too badly, and to his relief, he saw only a few small scratches. "Thank you, boy," Will said as he patted him gently on the head, careful not to touch any cuts.

"Our thanks, Vespasian," Fyodor said, strutting over to Will unscathed. "But time is of the essence, and we must get going."

"Of course, we understand," Vespasian said, and he flew down to the ground and landed gently next to Fyodor, who was just a bit taller. "Mountain Shadow Forest is near.

You should reach it in a couple hours. Once you get there, I recommend that you rest; tomorrow will be a long day, especially for you, William."

"William will rest," Fyodor said comfortingly. "I will watch over him tonight."

"You will all need your rest," Vespasian said, "and this army and I will watch over all of you tonight. So go, and when you reach the forest, stop and rest. We will be watching. But you must stay at the forest's edge, for we cannot enter the forest itself."

For a second, it looked as though Fyodor were going to object, but after a brief pause, he consented. "Thank you," he said, and then he turned to Liliu and Will. "Are you ready to travel, or do you need time to rest?"

Will stood, and Vespasian leaped into the air. "I'm ready," Will said. "And thank you, all of you, for helping me."

"Yeah," Liliu said. "Thanks."

"You are all welcome," Vespasian said, and Domitian and Constantine flew over, grabbed William's finger, and shook it. Then they did the same with Liliu and Fyodor. "We'll be watching."

Fyodor nodded, and they started out of the cave. Before they left, Liliu found her slingshot and picked it up, hopelessly looking at the broken string.

"Can you fix it?" Will asked.

"No," Liliu answered. "This kind of rope won't hold a knot."

"I'm sorry," Will said, and he put his hand on Liliu's shoulder after a moment's hesitation.

"It's okay. It did all that it could," Liliu said.

"It was a great help," Fyodor said.

After one last look, Liliu wrapped the rope around the base of the slingshot and then placed it back in her pocket. Will understood immediately; even though it was broken, it still held the last memory of her father, and in that way, it could never really be broken. So, after a comforting smile, Will, Liliu, Fyodor, and Spartacus left the cave. They had to squint in the light, but the warm air felt good, and by the look of the sun, it seemed to be late afternoon.

As the group made its way north over the rolling hills of green, a tremendous grogginess set in. For the next few hours, no more than five words were spoken among them. They all simply wanted to get to the forest's edge and sleep.

ELEVEN

AGAMEMNON

By the time they reached the edge of Mountain Shadow Forest, the sun had all but set. They probably could have gotten there faster had they not been so tired, but it didn't matter now, because they had arrived and were ready for a good night's sleep. Will and Liliu made a fire to combat the coming cold. When they were done, Liliu offered everyone a bit of food, but everyone, even Spartacus, was too tired to eat. Instead, they all curled up together, with Spartacus in the middle, and drifted off to sleep.

In front of Will, two huge wooden doors scarred with blackened burn marks opened to reveal a giant throne room crowded with mysterious monks in brown robes. Unable to stop himself, Will stepped into the room and scanned the giant walls that surrounded him. To his left and right were magnificently detailed paintings of Castle Village; the pictures had all the shops that he knew and even his home, with his father standing in the doorway. He could even find his friends, Louis and Bismarck, playing along one of the streets, and that was when he suddenly realized that Spartacus wasn't with him. He began to look around frantically, but his dog was nowhere near him, and then he spotted him in the painting, sitting next to an old barrel. Somehow, that seemed to be enough to calm Will down, and he was able to move forward once again.

After a few more steps, he reached the crowd of monks, who all took off their hoods, revealing the faces of all the people he had met so far on his journey. He saw Frederick, George, Liliu, and even the crooked sheriff. Then Will noticed a man he did not know hold up his hand in a gesture for Will to stop. Obediently, he came to a halt as the stranger approached. The man was tall and reminded him of Voltaire, but Will was convinced that it couldn't be him. When he reached Will, he held out his hand and placed a black piece of coal in William's palm. Then he took a breath to speak. William knew that this was going to be the question he had been waiting for, so the dark fragment in his hand must be the Millennium Stone. Will tilted his head slightly so that he was sure to hear the question, and the stranger spoke. But William couldn't understand him. He was speaking English, but the words didn't make any sense. They were real words, just thrown together in a nonsensical way. Again, the strange monk spoke, and again, Will couldn't understand what he was saying. His words were just gibberish. Then the room began to break into murmurs as the monks started to realize that Will did not have the answer. Frantically, Will asked them to repeat the question, but again, it made no sense. Will didn't know what to do; he was failing everyone, and then …

Will snapped awake. For a brief moment, he looked around anxiously at the trees and his friends until he finally realized where he was. *It was only a dream*, he thought to himself, and he let out a huge sigh of relief. Then he reached over and began to stroke Spartacus. The feel of his old friend immediately began to calm him down, at least enough to lie back down, but when he closed his eyes, the dream began to replay itself in his mind. After a moment of rolling from one side to the other, he gave in and sat up. Maybe he would try to eat, he thought, and he reached for a few nuts he had stashed in his pocket.

"Will, are you okay?" Liliu asked softly. "I can hear you tossing and turning."

Will rolled over and saw her sitting under the white glow of the moon. Her eyes had caught the pale moonlight and were shining it back at him as though they were made of bright blue stardust.

"I keep on dreaming about the monks and the question they're gonna ask me," Will said hopelessly.

Liliu lifted herself onto her elbow without breaking eye contact and then said compassionately, "Remember, Will, when you first told me about the question, and you said you didn't have an answer, so I said, 'Are you sure you're the one?'"

"Yeah," Will whispered solemnly.

"Well, I'm sure you're the one now," Liliu said with a small but encouraging smile. "We have been through too much for you not to be. Maybe if we had made it all this way and nothing had happened, then I would doubt that you're the one, because our adventure would have just been a hike. But it wasn't a hike; it was an adventure." Liliu paused and thought for a moment. "Do you understand what I'm saying?"

"I think so," Will said.

"It's like this," Liliu continued. "If this journey were easy, you wouldn't have the answer they're looking for. But because it was so hard, you will have the answer."

"Through conflict comes true understanding," Fyodor said groggily, and then he drifted right back to sleep.

Liliu and Will looked at each other with a smile, and then Will nodded. He was starting to get it, and more than that, he was starting to appreciate the journey. "Thank you, Liliu."

"You're welcome. Now, you should try to get a little sleep. I have a feeling that tomorrow's gonna be a long day."

Will smiled and laid his head down next to Spartacus. For the rest of the night, he slept soundly.

"William. William." Fyodor's voice roused him. "It is morning. Eat quickly; we should get moving soon."

Will nodded sleepily and then sat up and let his eyes adjust to the morning light.

"Here," Liliu said, and Will took a handful of nuts and berries from her.

"Thanks," he said lazily, and then he popped the first handful into his mouth. However, his crunching wasn't the only noise he heard. He looked down to find Spartacus chewing on a large bone.

"I took it from Fyodor's cottage," Liliu answered before Will could ask.

Will was happy that Liliu was helping to look after his best friend, so he thanked her with a smile before he turned to take in the forest behind him. Then he saw it—there in the distance was Mount Inkedu, towering above Mountain Shadow Forest. At the top, barely perceivable, was the white-and-black Temple of the Millennium Stone. Chewing slowly, he took in the entire view, from the deep-green forest that crept up the base of the mountain to the large, rolling gray clouds that hovered above the temple.

"Do not get caught up in appearances, William," Fyodor

cautioned, as if reading his mind. "Things often look much worse than they actually are."

Will nodded, finished his last handful of nuts, and strapped on his sword. As he stood, he patted his pocket gently to make sure he still had the potion and the crystal.

"I'm ready," Will said confidently, and the group all looked at him as Spartacus let out an encouraging bark. *It is time to defeat the Darkness.*

The four of them stepped into Mountain Shadow Forest. It was much denser than any other forest Will had ever been in, with all sorts of plant life, each one richly green. The trees were different as well. Unlike most trees, many there didn't shoot up into the sky; rather, they crawled along the ground like petrified snakes covered in moss, while others swirled into the air with giant spirals. Accompanying the luscious greens was an assortment of colorful flowers, from purples to reds to yellows. However, as beautiful as the flowers were, all the petals were starting to shrivel, and some had even begun to fall off.

"The forest is dying," Liliu said as a yellow petal fell gently at her feet from somewhere high above.

"It knows the Darkness is coming," Fyodor replied gloomily. Then he added as optimistically as he could, "But that's why we're here."

The group continued on, with Spartacus by William's side. They managed to find an area that seemed to be a path. *Maybe created by the monks,* William thought. It was wide enough for them to walk side by side. Only Will, Liliu, and Spartacus were walking now, as Fyodor had decided he could see more by sitting on Liliu's shoulder. The path twisted and wound its way around the large trees, but occasionally, Will and Liliu had to duck under the low-hanging branches. Then, just as they emerged around the bend of a particularly large tree, Spartacus began to growl, and it was no mystery why.

Lying in the path in front of them were the lifeless bodies of goblins. Their armor was broken, and the ground was stained with their thick, dark blood. Will pulled his sword immediately, as did Fyodor.

"Should we try to run through or go around?" William asked as his eyes searched the forest in front of them.

Before anyone could answer, something dropped from the tree above them and landed just feet from Will. Quickly, Will brought his sword up to strike, but the small blue creature with blue hair made up of blue flames did not move to defend himself, so Will froze. Then, from all around him, more small blue figures with burning hair emerged from the shadows of the forest. He saw both men and women, all dressed in black leather armor. Some were armed with long silver swords encrusted with deep-blue jewels, while others had extravagant white-gold bows with blue silk strings.

Will quickly realized that he was hopelessly outnumbered, so he lowered his sword, and the first creature he saw stepped closer. It wasn't till then that Will noticed his ears, which were long and pointy. *These are elves.*

"I couldn't imagine a more out-of-place group than this one," the elf said confidently. "One of you must be the one for whom we have been waiting."

"If you're talking about the one who is supposed to stop the Darkness," Will said, adding a hard swallow, "that's me."

The elf in front of him smiled widely, showing his gleaming white teeth. "It is good to see that you have made it. I am Iridium, a blue fire elf."

"My name is William," Will said. Then he pointed to his friends. "That's Liliu and Fyodor, and this is Spartacus," he said with a pat on the dog's head. He could see that Spartacus had no idea what to make of these new creatures.

"Hello to you all," Iridium said. "If you haven't guessed

it, we have been expecting you and have been keeping the road clear of those who would try to stop you."

"Thank you," Will said.

The elf smiled slightly, but the smile quickly faded. "Unfortunately, we have failed," he said, and his eyes fell to the ground. "Just ahead of you at the mountain path, a creature of the Darkness waits for you. We sent our bravest warriors against it, and they have all fallen. I'm sorry, William. It must be there for you to conquer."

William couldn't believe what he was hearing. These elves, who had killed more goblins than he could ever hope to defeat, couldn't kill something that he was going to have to face. He found himself speechless, but luckily, Liliu had her wits about her.

"Thank you for trying," she said sympathetically. "I'm sorry that you lost your friends."

"Do not be sorry," Iridium said calmly. "They were warriors. To live alongside evil was not something that they could do."

"True warriors indeed," Fyodor added, and the elf nodded as though a talking frog were something he had seen many times.

"However, we will not send you against it defenseless," Iridium said with a new power in his voice. "Come now—let me see what weapons you possess."

Will went first and held out the sword that Fyodor had given him. Iridium looked it over with a close eye. His fiery blue hair burned close to Will, but he felt no heat from it. After looking from one end of the blade to the other, he stood and said, "That is a fine sword; there is nothing that needs to be done to it."

Out of the corner of his eye, Will could see Fyodor stand a little taller. Then Iridium moved on to Liliu.

"And you," he said. "What weapon do you possess?"

"My weapon is broken," Liliu said sadly as she pulled her slingshot from her back pocket and presented it to the elf.

Iridium took it gently in his hands and then smiled compassionately at Liliu. "There is much love in this; keep it with you always. But its time as a weapon has ended," Iridium said. Then he called out over his shoulder, "Samarium!" A tall, slender female elf with long blue flames that burned from her scalp and then flowed smoothly down her back stepped forward and held out a long white-gold bow for Liliu to take. Hesitantly, Liliu reached out for it, and when the elf did not withdraw, Liliu took it into her hand.

"Thank you," Liliu said, examining its smooth edges.

Samarium nodded and then handed her five golden arrows and returned to the forest. Liliu glanced over at Will, and he smiled at her. He couldn't think of a better weapon for her.

Finally, Iridium turned to Fyodor, who jumped from Liliu's shoulder and drew Will's sword with pride. The elf meticulously looked over the blade, first with his right eye and then with his left. For some reason, Will found himself getting a little nervous, as though his skills were being put to the test. He was greatly relieved when he saw the elf smile slightly.

"This blade was made with great care, and it is truly strong, but we will make it stronger." With that, Iridium walked to another elf, who handed him a small vial of a glowing blue liquid. Iridium took the vial and the sword William had made and then poured the thick elixir over it. As it ran down the blade, it burned with light-blue flames until it reached the hilt and vanished. "Now it is unbreakable and will remain so until dawn tomorrow." Then he handed the sword back to Fyodor, who took it with care. "Now you are ready," the elf added confidently.

"Sir," William said, "do you have anything for Spartacus?"

This question made the elf smile once again. "You have

all that you need for him," Iridium said. Then he added with a nod, "Trust in that."

Will didn't know what he was talking about but was not about to question him. He just nodded.

"Now, carry on," Iridium declared, and he stepped aside. "We will ensure that the path behind you stays clear."

"Thank you," Fyodor said. Then he jumped back onto Liliu's shoulder.

Will felt a great swell of gratitude but could not find the words, so he simply nodded again, and they marched on. The elves watched them pass, and some saluted, but as brave as they thought he was, he felt like a coward because deep inside, fear was starting to boil over. He wanted now more than ever to run back home. After all he'd been through, he had never felt as if he were marching into battle, not even against the pixies, although marching into battle might have been exactly what he was doing from the start.

In silence, they passed through the forest, and the closer they got to the mountain, the more Will wanted to flee. But something kept him going. Although he wasn't sure, it seemed that his companions' strength pushed him on, especially that of Spartacus, who went wherever Will went, because that was where Will needed him. That was really all Will was doing: going where everybody needed him to go. And perhaps he needed his friends where they were, and that was why they were there. Will was right where he needed to be, and that thought gave him strength. It was enough to push him on to the mountain path.

As they walked, Will fumbled with the dragon crystal in his pocket. He figured this was probably the time to break it, but he needed to be sure. If he had broken it every time he had been scared, he wouldn't have it now.

All Will could hear were the soft footsteps of his companions and himself as they continued down the dirt path. The path wound between shrubs and around trees. He sensed that the mountain was getting close, and that meant so was the creature the elves had mentioned. Will looked at Liliu and could tell she was as scared as he was, but he knew she would never admit it—not because of pride but to give him strength. With a pat on the back, Will let her know that he was thankful for her being there.

Just ahead, the trail made a final turn, and as they came around the bend, Will saw him—the creature that the Darkness had sent to kill him. He was a nightmare—at least seven feet tall, with a twisted crown of bone that tangled upward from the top of his skull. The skin on his face and arms was light gray with black veins that ran just below the surface. Beyond that, the creature seemed to have two sets of wings; one set, like a bat's wings, were folded around his shoulders like a cape. His second set, which were feathered and black like a raven's wings, were stretched out behind him. Dull black armor covered his chest and legs, and in his right hand, he held a black steel ax with veins of red ruby. The weapon was as tall as the creature itself. All around the wicked creature were the bodies of the blue fire elves who had tried to stop him; their hair was no longer ablaze. When the dark figure saw Will and the others emerge in front of him, he did not move; he just watched them with his deep black eyes. Will took the lead. After taking a few more steps, he stopped a good distance from the dark figure and drew his sword.

"Finally." The creature's voice rolled like thunder as he took his ax with both hands. "Your death will usher in a new era of darkness."

"Identify yourself, assassin," Fyodor ordered fearlessly as he leaped from Liliu's shoulder to the ground in front of Will and drew his own sword, "so that we may put your failure in the history books."

"Such impudence," the evil creature roared. "I am the claws of the Darkness and the destroyer of hope and beauty. I am an eternity of despair. I am Agamemnon!"

"To arms, my friends!" Fyodor yelled, and Liliu readied an arrow as Will raised his sword. "Prepare yourself, fiend, for I am Fyodor, destroyer of despair!"

With that, Fyodor lunged. Will could tell that he took Agamemnon off guard. The creature had no doubt expected to make the first move, but it was too late—Fyodor was flying through the air. He thrust his sword forward, but Agamemnon dodged at the last minute by dropping his shoulder and sending Fyodor sailing over him. Spartacus was the next to attack. In a flash of movement, he leaped from the ground and clinched his jaw around Agamemnon's right forearm. In a cry of rage, the shadowy beast flung Spartacus from his arm and into the bushes; thick black blood oozed from the puncture holes in his arm. Will was about to advance, when Agamemnon let out a roar and unfurled all four wings to their greatest span.

"Enough!" Agamemnon cried. "You will all die!" Furiously, he spun around with his ax and slammed it into the ground near Fyodor, who was just standing. The frog jumped away at the last second. Not wanting to hesitate any longer, Will charged. But Agamemnon was ready and swung his ax back toward him. Will managed to block it, but the sheer force of the blow knocked him back into Liliu and sent them both to the ground. Then the dark creature raised his ax to finish Will, but Fyodor leaped onto his back and jammed the sword into his shoulder. Again, Agamemnon screamed, letting the ax fall. Will barely managed to roll away. Angrier now than ever, the beast reached up to grab Fyodor, but again, the frog hopped away.

In the commotion, Liliu jumped to her feet, reloaded her first arrow, and fired it over Will. With a zip, it ricocheted off Agamemnon's armor and stuck in the ground. This immediately caught Agamemnon's attention, and he advanced on her, but Will wasn't going to let him touch her. He jumped to his feet and moved between Liliu and the dark beast just as Fyodor cut another gash into Agamemnon's right arm. This time, Agamemnon ignored him and raised his ax. Just as Will brought his sword up to block the ax, he felt one of the creature's wings strike his legs and knock him flat on his back. As soon as he fell, Liliu fired again, this time aiming for Agamemnon's head. Unfortunately, Agamemnon flinched, and the arrow slipped by his cheek and then ripped into the skin of his left bat wing. With a roar, he charged Liliu. Fyodor leaped, and Will shot to his feet, but they were both swept aside by the beast's wings. With a furious speed, Agamemnon grabbed Liliu's bow and ripped it from her hands just as she tried to load another arrow. Savagely, he struck her across the face with it, casting her to the ground unconscious.

Will darted up once again, grabbed Liliu's shirt, and pulled her away as fast as he could before Agamemnon could finish her off. Fyodor made another pass, cutting across the dark creature's exposed left arm. Agamemnon had had enough. He began swinging his huge ax wildly at Fyodor, but his heavy movements weren't quick enough to catch him. Fyodor leaped all around, cutting and slashing wherever he could. Some cuts sliced across his arms, while others zipped across Agamemnon's armored breastplate.

Once Liliu was safely aside, Will turned back toward the fight. He knew that Fyodor could not keep jumping around forever. It was time to break the crystal and call the dragon to him. As Will reached into his pocket, Fyodor made a jump for Agamemnon's head. But Agamemnon ducked and whirled at the same time, popping his wings out and forward. Will watched in horror as the bony part of Agamemnon's feathered wing struck Fyodor and sent him somersaulting through the air. His fragile frog body slammed into a tree and then dropped limply into the dying leaves of a small bush.

"No!" Will cried, and he yanked the small red crystal from his pocket. But just as he was about to toss it to the ground to break it, Agamemnon grabbed his wrist and tore it from his fingers.

"What is this?" Agamemnon said, seemingly calm now that Will's three friends had been dealt with. "A weapon perhaps? Foolish boy," he said with an evil grin. Then he dropped the crystal to the ground and slammed the bottom of his ax into it, shattering it into tiny pieces.

After watching the crystal shatter, Will looked up into Agamemnon's dark eyes and raised his sword to the ready. The crystal dragon was coming, and Will knew in his heart that Agamemnon was no match for the two of them.

Agamemnon raised his ax, and the red sapphire veins gleamed in the shadows. Then he set himself into a low fighting stance and took a deep breath through his nose. "I can smell your fear, boy, and it is making my mouth water." Agamemnon suddenly swung, and Will jumped back, but the ax caught the tip of his sword, sending vibrations ringing through the entire blade.

Will remembered what Fyodor had told him: defend and counter. So again, he raised his sword to the ready, and Agamemnon took a step forward.

"You are no match for me," Agamemnon said. "Give in to despair; it is the only true nature of the world." Again, Agamemnon swung, but this time, Will ducked and swung back. Reacting immediately, Agamemnon whirled the long handle of the weapon around, blocked Will's blow, and then slashed again with the ax. The huge black blade collided with Will's sword, sending him stumbling back, but he regained his balance quickly, and to his surprise, he was swinging again. Agamemnon blocked two of the strikes with his ax, but the third hit his fingers. Enraged, Agamemnon went on the offensive without regard for himself. He swung the ax once, barely missing Will, and then whirled it around his head and sent it hurtling back toward Will again. Luckily, it was a clumsy swing, and the flat part of the blade slammed into Will. Will could feel his entire body jerk on impact, and he flew back and slammed hard into the ground. His sword tumbled away from him.

Painfully, he looked up at the dark-winged beast that stood over him. His body hurt too much to move. All he could do was watch Agamemnon raise his ax over his head and prepare to strike. But then he heard it—like the cry of a thousand crystal glasses humming in harmony. The crystal dragon had arrived. It burst through the treetops and slammed into Agamemnon with the force of twenty horses, driving him to the earth. Agamemnon looked up at the crystal dragon in dismay as the dragon's sparkling blue-green eyes bore into the darkness of Agamemnon's.

Unfortunately, Agamemnon's surprise vanished quickly. With a powerful thrust of his wings, he cast the dragon off him and propelled himself to his feet. In the open forest, Agamemnon and the crystal dragon circled. Will could see pure hatred etched on the dark creature's face, and again, he raised his ax to strike, but the dragon lunged first, catching the handle of the ax in its mouth. With roars bellowing from each side, the two wrestled for the blade, and Will realized that his part in this fight was not finished. Painfully, he forced himself to his feet and darted for his sword.

Agamemnon managed to yank his ax free and sent the blade crashing into the dragon's side, causing a shower of glowing crystals to explode into the air. The dragon let out a roar that forced Will's hands to his ears, and then it swung around and used its long, jagged tail to slash into Agamemnon's face. Thick black blood began to drip from

Agamemnon's cheek, but again, he raised his ax and swung. This time, the dragon dropped, flattening its body against the ground, and the ax sailed over.

By now, Will had found his sword, and he was ready to join the dragon, but Agamemnon saw him and unfurled his wings, no doubt preparing to defend his back. Undeterred, Will charged. With a flick of his bat wing, Agamemnon struck Will in the chest, sending him tumbling back. But that left an opening for the crystal dragon. It lunged forward, driving its claws into the dark creature's armor, forcing him back against the trunk of a large tree. Agamemnon reacted with surprising finesse as he twirled his ax over the arms of the crystal dragon and then shoved the blade into its throat. Will could hear crystals starting to break as the dark creature pushed on his ax, but the dragon was not letting go. Then, with a tremendous jerk, the crystal dragon tore the armored breastplate from Agamemnon, leaving his chest bare. Just feet away, Will jumped to his feet, and as Agamemnon forced the crystal dragon to the ground with a powerful shove, Will lunged in a leap of faith and desperation. With his eyes closed, he felt the tip of the sword pierce Agamemnon's flesh, and then, suddenly, everything went quiet.

Slowly, Will opened his eyes. In an eerie silence, the dark creature stumbled sideways with the sword still in his chest and began melting away into a thick black goo. The look on his face was one of disbelief, as if he had just realized that perhaps hope could defeat despair. Unfortunately, in the black mess, as the beast melted away, so did the sword. Will could only watch, as though he were hypnotized, until the last remnants of the beast had dissolved into a puddle of thick black liquid that quickly turned to ash and blew away. Backing up, Will saw the crystal dragon bring itself slowly to its feet and turn to look at Will.

"Are you hurt?" the dragon asked in its usual crystal harmony.

"Not too badly," Will said, feeling the shoulder that Agamemnon had struck with his ax. The injury had faded from a sharp pain to a dull ache.

"And your companion, the dog?" the dragon said.

But before Will could answer, Liliu sat up, and the dragon backed away to get a better look at her.

"Liliu!" Will cried. "Are you okay?"

"I think so," she replied, rubbing her forehead. "But I have a huge headache."

Will ran to her side and helped her up, and then he found that he couldn't stop himself from giving her a hug.

"Where's Fyodor and Spa ..." Liliu trailed off the moment she saw the large, colorful crystal dragon resting in front of her.

"Liliu, this is the crystal dragon I told you about, the one who would come when the crystal was broken."

"Oh," Liliu murmured shyly as she looked up into its swirling blue-green eyes.

Just then, another bush rustled, and a bewildered Fyodor came stumbling out of it. "Did we win?" he asked, looking up at Will, Liliu, and the dragon.

"Yes," Will said, but then he added sadly, "I don't know where Spartacus is. And this is the crystal dragon."

"Yes, I heard," Fyodor said. "Not to be rude, but we must find our missing friend."

Will was glad to hear him say that, and the group, including the dragon, fanned out. However, it didn't take long for Will to find him. He was behind a large shrub next to a tree, lying still.

"Spartacus!" Will cried, and he dropped to his knees beside him. The others rushed over immediately.

"Oh no!" Liliu shrieked, placing her hand thoughtfully on Will's shoulder.

Will gently brushed Spartacus's face and then felt his chest for any signs of a heartbeat. Like a feather drumming against his hand, he could feel Spartacus's life fading. Tears swelled in Will's eyes and poured over onto his cheeks.

"I'm sorry, Will," Fyodor said with all the empathy in him. "It's Agamemnon's blood. It must be a horrible poison."

Will looked down and saw the black blood from Agamemnon's arm draining from Spartacus's mouth, and a tear fell from his face and splashed in the dark blood. Then a great hope leaped inside of Will as he remembered the potion he'd bought at Potemkin Village. This was what it was for—it had to be! Frantically, he reached inside his pocket and pulled the vial out. Then, carefully, he pulled the top off and lowered it to Spartacus's lips. Liliu, Fyodor, and the dragon watched closely as Will poured the clear liquid into his faithful companion's mouth. A long moment passed during which nothing happened, but Will did not lose hope. Even when Liliu squeezed his shoulder as if to tell him to give up, he wouldn't. And then, with a soft woof, Spartacus opened his eyes and began licking William's hand. Will was now crying harder than ever, tears of great joy. Liliu exploded into laughter, and Fyodor let out a triumphant roar. Even the great crystal dragon was smiling.

"You're gonna be just fine, boy," Will said, and when Spartacus sat up, he gave him a tremendous hug. He was now ready to face the monks of Mount Inkedu.

TWELVE

THE MILLENNIUM STONE

William was at the base of the mountain path, looking up with his head cranked all the way back. The top of Mount Inkedu had disappeared into the clouds, taking the monastery with it, which meant that Will would have to venture into the clouds. But with his friends by his side, he felt as if he could do anything.

"William," the crystal dragon said in a low, harmonic tone, "I'm afraid this is as far as we can go."

Will couldn't help but look a bit puzzled. He thought that maybe the dragon had meant it would have to go. *But why did it say "we"?*

"William, he's right," Fyodor said. "The rest of this journey is yours. We cannot help you any longer."

"What?" Will shot back. "You helped me this far; what if I need you up there?"

"The foes you will face up there," the dragon said, looking to the clouds, "are not the kinds of foes that we can fight for you. But have faith in yourself, William; you can defeat them."

"You're talking about the question, aren't you?" Will said, looking down at Fyodor. He realized that he had never gotten to ask the frog what the answer could be. "But I have no idea what to say."

"You will," Fyodor replied, looking up at him. "Listen to your heart, and be honest in everything you say, and you will have all the answers that you seek."

Will looked at Liliu, who had been unusually quiet, and the look on her face said everything: she had faith in him too, as they all did. But for some reason, it mattered most to Will that she did.

"Can Spartacus come with me?"

"I'm afraid not," Fyodor said. "But we will look after him here."

Liliu squatted down next to Spartacus and put her arm around his shoulder. "You have to stay here, Spartacus," she said. "But William will be back soon." Spartacus let out a low whine but stayed put.

Will had nothing more to say. Slowly, his eyes swept past each one of his companions as they looked back confidently. With a nod to all of them, Will turned, but before he could take his first step, he heard Liliu call his name from behind him. Will turned, and Liliu was there. She threw her arms around him and gave him a tremendous hug. For a second, Will was so stunned that he just stood there like a statue, but when she didn't let go, Will wrapped his arms around her and squeezed back. When they finally let go, Liliu was blushing a deep red, and she obviously knew it, because she quickly hid her head and darted back over to Spartacus. William couldn't help but smile as he turned back toward the mountain, and with a deep breath, he started upward.

William had to fight the urge to glance back as he ascended the crumbling stone steps, which were horribly uneven; some steps were inches apart, while others were well over a foot high. Also, the stone staircase zigzagged up the mountain rather than spiraling around it, which, for some reason, was how William had always imagined it. However, because of the steps' design, it seemed as if he were making faster progress, and soon he was looking down on the treetops of the forest.

It didn't take long for Will's legs to start burning with every step, but he refused to stop. He was determined to push on for as long as he could. Turning left, he started another series of stairs. Now he was high above the trees, and when he looked out, he could see Death Basin in the distance. A cool breeze brushed against his skin, and as he turned to another set of stairs, he looked up and saw the bottom of the clouds, which weren't far away now. Will had often wondered what it would be like to touch a cloud, so he pushed a little faster with the hope that the clouds wouldn't suddenly blow away before he got a chance to touch them.

Luckily, the clouds had barely moved by the time he got to them. Slowly, he reached up, and just as his fingertips began to touch the wisps of a cloud, he swirled his hand and watched the cloud spiral around his hand. Then Will stepped into the cloud itself. He could feel the temperature drop immediately as the cool mist settled on his skin. However, now in the dense fog, William could see the light glow of the monastery above him. It was still far away, but Will was happy to have a beacon to guide him.

With the muscles in his legs on fire, Will ascended the last steps until he came to the huge entrance doors to the monastery. They were nothing like the ones in his dream. They were much bigger and were made of marble, not wood. On the door itself was a beautiful sculpting of two large warriors in monks' robes, holding long golden spears that crossed at the break between the two doors. The beautiful white marble, however, was stained with dust and other blackened filth, which managed to take away from the warrior's ferocity.

Will looked around for a rope or some kind of bell he could ring to let the monks know he had arrived, but he found none. He decided that as hopeless as it seemed, he would try to knock. But just as he raised his hand, he heard the huge stone doors shift and then start to slide back as they scraped across the marble floor.

Standing on the other side was a monk, and to Will's disappointment, he looked as dirty as those carved into the door. His robe, which completely covered his head and body, was stained with streaks of black soot that started densely at his shoulders and then faded as they made their way to his feet. Patiently, the monk waited for the doors to slide to a halt, and then he slowly and methodically waved Will forward with his sleeve. Cautiously, Will stepped into the temple and followed the monk down a long, dimly lit hall that had the entire drama of the Darkness's last attack on the kingdom carved into it. There were people running in fear and cities burning. Elves and dragons were being devoured by the Darkness, but then, at the end of the hall, the carving showed a boy no older than William, holding something he couldn't see because of the grime that covered it. But whatever it was, the Darkness was afraid of it. *It must be the Millennium Stone,* Will thought.

At the end of the hall, another pair of doors opened, this time to an immense, circular room with a ceiling that looked as if it were a hundred feet high. Inside, it seemed as though all the monks had gathered, standing in their filthy robes. As William passed them, he could see their faces deep within their hoods. Their skin was gray, and their cheeks were sunken in; they had thin black lips and sickly yellow eyes that watched in shame as William passed. Many tried to hide their faces altogether, and not one of them dared to speak. In fact, the room was unnervingly quiet. Instead, they all simply pointed at once to the center of the room. Reluctantly, Will looked to the middle and saw a large, concave marble rock beneath a thick, glossy black stone hovering in the middle of everyone.

"The Millennium Stone," Will said more to himself than to the monks around him, but they all answered with nods. Will could feel his heart start to pound in his chest. He knew the question was coming, and he was trying to clear his mind, but they weren't saying anything. So Will waited, and after a long moment, the monk who had led him in looked at him awkwardly until, finally, he spoke.

"What are you waiting for?" he said in a raspy voice.

"Your question," Will answered, puzzled.

A low mumbling began to roll through the crowd of monks until one of them silenced everyone with a loud "Shhh!" Then he spoke to Will in the same raspy voice the other monk had used. "What question do you speak of?"

"The question that you have for me," Will said uncomfortably, immediately realizing how foolish that statement sounded. Again, a series of whispers grew in the room until the monk silenced them again.

"Our question," the monk said, this time in a condescending tone, "is how do we reawaken the Millennium Stone?"

Will could not have been hit harder had the monk punched him. He had come all this way to a question he hadn't the slightest clue how to answer. *How could the king have thought I would know? How could the wizard have put me in this position?* Anger started to boil up in him, and the monks must have sensed it, because they burst into desperate rants. They were no longer mumbling but screaming and crying to one another that the end was near, and now everything was hopeless. But in their whimpering, Will felt something burst inside of him: faith and determination. He hadn't come this far to give up now, and he could not believe that the protectors of such a magical stone would give up so easily. They had put all their hope in William and had stopped trying to figure out a solution for themselves. Suddenly, anger exploded in William, and he yelled at everyone, "Enough! Listen to yourselves. You're supposed to be protecting everybody, but you've all given up!"

"There is nothing we can do!" one of the monks called out desperately from the other side of the room. "The stone is broken!"

"It is not broken!" Will shot back. "You have allowed the magic to fade away!"

"All things fade away; all things die," a voice whimpered from the back. "That's the way of things."

Will couldn't believe what he was hearing. All these people had let the Darkness in before it had even arrived in the kingdom. The Darkness started right there—not outside of the kingdom but within it, just as before, all because these monks had forgotten that it took courage to live a good life. Hope was something for the brave, and these monks had become cowards. "You should all be ashamed!" Will screamed. "My friends and I had to fight to get here. My dog almost died! And yes, one day, he will die, but not today, because I didn't give up—so now I will get to see him again. But if the Darkness comes and destroys everything, then I'll never be able to see him again, and some people will never exist and never be able to pet a dog or meet a girl named Liliu. And for all that death takes away, I would rather experience life than never feel anything at all, so life is worth fighting for, and it's worth living!"

Suddenly, the stone began to fizzle, and blue sparks started to burst from its surface. Will spun around to face the stone, and the moment he did, it burst into bright blue flames. The monks had to hide their eyes, but Will looked directly into it.

"He has done it," one of the monks said, awestruck, and Will could see him on the other side of the room, trying to look at the burning Millennium Stone.

"But how?" another asked, still cowering from the light.

"Courage and faith," the first monk replied, standing as tall as he could and facing the stone, allowing its rays to burn away the ash that covered his robe. Slowly, Will could see the robe begin to brighten, and even the monk's skin started to color. Then others started to join him, and soon almost everyone was facing the stone and feeling its warmth. Then the monk who had just spoken approached Will and said calmly, "Thank you. You have reminded us of our purpose, of everyone's purpose: to preserve life. As long as there is life, there is hope! Now you must take the stone and go back to Castle Village. The Darkness will be there soon."

"But how can I get there? It's many miles from here," Will said.

"There is someone outside who can take you. And tell him that we are sorry we let him down as well," the monk said. Then he gestured to the long hallway that led to the front entrance.

Will nodded his thanks and then confidently reached out and took the burning stone into his hand. It wasn't much bigger than his own fist, and it felt as though a cool breeze were blowing in his hand. Then he turned and raced down the hall. As he approached the doors, they opened, revealing the crystal dragon, who was smiling at its brave new friend.

"Excellent work, William. But now it is time to defeat the Darkness itself. Hop on; I will take you there myself," the dragon said, spinning around and lowering a wing for Will to climb onto. Without a word, Will jumped onto his back, and the dragon leaped from the mountaintop and into the air.

THIRTEEN

DARKNESS FALLS

Sitting on the crystal dragon wasn't comfortable, but after a few seconds of soaring through the air, high above the treetops, Will forgot about the crystals poking him in the legs. It was amazing how much faster the dragon could travel. In only a couple of minutes, they had cleared Mountain Shadow Forest, and they were now gliding over Death Basin. Besides the wind in his hair, it felt as though a cool breeze were washing over his left arm and chest, where he held the Millennium Stone tightly. Meanwhile, his right arm was precariously holding on to the dragon, but he wasn't the least bit worried. He knew that the dragon would never let him fall.

"Crystal dragon?" Will said coyly, not sure what else he was supposed to call the creature. The name seemed to work, because it turned its head slightly toward Will. "How did you know I was going to be able to do it?"

"You mean revive the Millennium Stone?" the dragon replied calmly.

"Yeah."

"I didn't."

"What?" Will shouted into the wind. "You seemed to know from the start."

"I had an idea that it was you, but humans are so unpredictable," the dragon said, and Will could feel the air in his face push harder against him as the dragon accelerated slightly. "It was your confidence and humility that caught my attention, William. I have met many who were confident and many who were humble, but it is truly rare to find one who is both. Do not lose that. It is a great strength."

"Humble confidence," Will repeated.

"Exactly," the dragon said, and they started to fly over Witchwick Marsh. All Will could see was a dense white mist with the occasional shimmer of dark water beneath it, but as much as he searched, he couldn't find any sign of the small witch village from which he and the others had escaped. Almost playfully, the dragon swooped down and glided just above the marsh, and the mist swirled around him.

With amazing speed, they crossed the marshes, and in the distance, Will could see the tall trees of Skyreach Forest as the crystal dragon climbed into the air. Above the trees, a pack of harpies was swirling in patterns around one another, but the moment they saw the crystal dragon, they all frantically shot down into the treetops. *It's nice to see creatures running away from me for once.*

As they passed Skyreach Forest, Will knew that they were getting close. In the distance, he could see Potemkin. The village looked as if it were in a frenzy; people were running around anxiously. It seemed everyone was packing to leave the town as fast as he or she could, and with a quick glance to the left, he understood why. In the distance, he could see the Darkness—a cloud of blackness creeping slowly over the land, a void of despair and death stalking the people.

"I will try to take you as close as I can, William," the dragon roared. "Hold on tight!"

With a last push, the dragon raced over the crystal canyon and the rolling hills to Castle Village. Will's heart jumped when he saw that the castle was still standing, but the Darkness was nearly on top of it. Below, a crowd of people was fleeing across the plains. Many were on horses, and some were on foot, but all stopped when they saw the crystal dragon fly overhead. Some began to cheer, and Will held up the Millennium Stone for everyone to see. He wanted everyone to know that it would be all right. Then a blast of ice-cold air hit William, nearly knocking him off the dragon as they were both thrust back. Holding to its promise to get Will as close as it could, the crystal dragon lowered its head and dived beside the hill next to Castle Village, where Will had been when he had first seen the Darkness.

"Hold on, Will!" the crystal dragon roared again, and Will sank down tightly against its crystal-edged body. The dragon cut close to the castle, and standing on one of the ledges was King Herodotus. As the dragon zoomed by him, the king smiled. Will wanted to smile back, but dust from the mountain was showering onto his face, forcing him to tuck his chin and seal his eyes shut.

With a shudder, the dragon crashed into the ground. The impact sent Will plummeting to the dirt. As his body tumbled across the ground, the Millennium Stone slipped from his grip and rolled toward the shadowy darkness. Immediately, an icy wind slammed into Will's body and tried to force him off the hill, but he dug his fingers into the ground and managed to stay low enough so that most of the wind sailed over him. However, the strong gust caught the crystal dragon's wings and thrust it off the mountain, and it tumbled through the air. It disappeared into a haze of dust and dirt.

Furious at what he had just seen, Will dug his fingers deep in the ground and began clawing his way to the stone, but the Darkness was onto him. Long black claws began to form in the clouds above, and then, with tremendous speed, they reached from the sky straight for him. He jumped forward with all his might, and the claws just missed, slamming into the ground near him. They threw debris high into the air, and it rained back down around him. Then a scream, high pitched and angry, tore from the sky above him, and Will looked up just in time to see a huge hand with bony black fingers and sharp, shadowy nails reach for him. Thinking quickly, Will pushed off the ground, letting the wind slam into his chest and thrust him backward, causing the hand to narrowly miss. Instead, it got a handful of dirt and dry grass and then vanished into a smoky mist that blew furiously past him.

Digging in once again, Will fought forward. More black spikes fell from the sky, forcing Will to roll left and right across the rocky ground. No matter what the Darkness threw at him, Will pushed forward until the Millennium Stone was only an arm's length away. Then, just as William reached for the stone, the Darkness made one last attempt to blow William off the mountain, but the gust struck the stone first and pushed it into William's hands. He clutched it tightly and immediately felt a new strength. He pushed himself to his feet, the wind raging futilely against him.

Grasping the stone tightly in his right hand, he raised it to the black clouds above. The Darkness formed into a giant mouth with huge fangs that crashed down around him, but Will did not flinch. The Darkness started to swirl around him, angry and roaring, but the Millennium Stone shone brighter than ever. Its blue flames unfurled around him, shot into the sky, and exploded into a burning embrace that consumed the Darkness and then erupted into streaks of fiery lightning that obliterated all traces of the black cloud. In an instant, the Darkness was vanquished and replaced by a warm sun and a clear blue sky that stretched out over rolling hills of wheat.

Slowly, Will lowered the Millennium Stone, which was still burning in soft blue flames, to his side. A gentle breeze touched his face as he faintly began to hear the roar of a cheering crowd. As he turned back to the village, he saw everyone celebrating. People were dancing in the streets and jumping for joy throughout the town. Only then did Will realize he had done it. The Darkness was gone!

With a grin growing across his cheeks, Will raced down the hill to the celebration below. He couldn't wait to see his dad and tell him all about his adventures. But just before he reached the bottom of the hill, he remembered the crystal dragon, and his eyes shot upward. However, he saw nothing but blue sky. In all the excitement, a hint of sadness touched his heart, but he returned his gaze to the sea of people rushing toward him, and the words *humble confidence* echoed in his mind. More calmly, he headed into the crowd.

His dad was the first person to reach him, and he swept Will up in his arms with a giant kiss on the cheek. "William, you did it!" he yelled triumphantly, and then he set him back down, beaming. Will didn't know what to say. He could only smile as friends and strangers approached him and began to pat him on the back or shake his hand. Then the crowd suddenly began to part and bow as King Herodotus and the great wizard Voltaire approached. Will took a knee.

"Oh no, please," the king said humbly. "You have earned the right to stand among kings."

Hearing that, Will stood slowly, and the king placed his hand on William's shoulder.

"You have done greatly," the king continued. "You deserve to be honored among the heroes of old. From this day forth," the king said loudly, turning to the crowd, "today will be a holiday in celebration of young William's courage. He and he alone—" Suddenly, the king paused and looked around. "Where is your dog?"

"He's okay, Your Majesty. He's at Mount Inkedu, waiting for me," Will answered.

"Oh, very good to hear," King Herodotus said, and then

he turned back to the crowd. "As I was saying, he and he alone, with only his—"

"Your Majesty," William interrupted meekly, "I wasn't alone. I actually had help."

"Help, you say?" Voltaire asked.

"Yes, sir. From people I met along the way. I know that I was supposed to be alone, but I couldn't have done it without them."

"Who were these people?" the king asked, turning back to Will.

"There was a girl named—" Suddenly, Will was interrupted by a giant gasp from the crowd. When he looked up, his heart jumped—the crystal dragon had returned with his friends on its back. Everyone parted as quickly as possible to give the dragon room to land, and Will ran over to it and threw his arms around its neck. "How did you make it back so fast?"

"The Millennium Stone is much heavier than you make it seem, William," the dragon said, and the next thing Will knew, Spartacus jumped into his arms, knocking him to the ground, and began licking his face relentlessly. Luckily, Liliu was there to rescue him, and she extended a hand to help him up. Will thanked her with a smile and noticed that her eyes were fixed on the Millennium Stone.

"Is that it—the Millennium Stone?" she asked.

"Yeah," Will answered. "It destroyed the Darkness."

"No, William," the dragon said. "You destroyed the Darkness."

Then someone from the crowd yelled, "Three cheers for William!" And then everyone, even the king, broke into the chant: "Hip hip hooray! Hip hip hooray! Hip hip hooray!"

"No," William said, smiling at Liliu. "*We* destroyed the Darkness."

The dragon broke into a laughter that broke the harmony

of its voice for the first time, which made the crowd step back and cover their ears.

Once the dragon was done laughing, the king stepped forward and addressed Will once again. "And who are your friends, William?"

"Well, Your Majesty," Will said, "this is Liliu Okkalnin."

"Liliu Okalani, Your Majesty," she said, correcting him, and the king bowed slightly.

"And, Dad," William said, suddenly turning to his father, "she doesn't have a place to live, so can she stay with us?"

John glanced at Liliu, grinned, and then said warmly, "Of course."

With a bout of laughter, William and Liliu embraced. "We are gonna have so much fun," Will said as they separated. Then Will turned back to the king. "And this is the crystal dragon," Will said, stepping to the side so that they could properly meet.

"Your Majesty," the dragon said, and the king bowed lower than Will had ever seen him bow.

"Thank you for your service, dragon," the king said. "I realize that we have not respected your lands as we should have. Consider that issue now remedied."

The dragon responded with a nod, and then, before Will could continue, Fyodor stepped forward. The king looked curiously down at him. "Your Majesty, it is I, Fyodor Dostoevsky."

"Fyodor!" the king blurted out with a grin. "I should have known that you would have had a hand in this. What happened to you, my old friend?"

"Witches, Your Majesty; they have cursed me."

Smiling, Voltaire stepped forward and drew his wand from his robe. Then, in growing circles, he began spiraling the wand over Fyodor's green head until streaks of gold zipped around him. As Voltaire raised his wand, Fyodor began to stretch and widen as he returned to his human form, complete with a beautiful set of garments.

"Fyodor!" Will and Liliu said at the same time, and Liliu gave him a big hug. The tall, slender, gray-haired man, complete with deep-green garments and sparkling green eyes, smiled widely as he was welcomed back to his human form.

"Thank you, Voltaire," Fyodor said. "You are truly a great wizard."

Voltaire just nodded and then dropped to a knee and began examining the Millennium Stone closely. "So, William," Voltaire said, "what do you suppose we should do with this?"

"Keep it at the monastery, sir," William told him confidently. "We can trust it with them again. I'm sure of it."

"That's all I needed to hear," the king said. "Then there is one last quest for you, to take the stone back. You can leave tomorrow, but now you will have a full escort."

"That will not be necessary, Your Majesty," the crystal dragon said politely. "I will take him back myself, as soon as William is ready."

"Excellent, and thank you again," King Herodotus said. Then he turned back to the crowd one final time and yelled, "Let the celebrations begin!" With that, the entire village broke into cheers and songs. William and Liliu spent the rest of the night playing and celebrating as Will showed her around town. The king offered William and his father a place to live in the castle, which John humbly declined, but he said that he would be happy to visit. The next day, the dragon flew Will and Liliu to the temple, which the monks were hard at work cleaning, and Will placed the Millennium Stone back in its rightful place. From there, the dragon gave them a ride all around the kingdom until they were both so tired and hungry that they had to return to Castle Village, where John had a huge meal ready for both of them, and they lived happily ever after.

Printed in the USA
CPSIA information can be obtained
at www.ICGtesting.com
LVHW042027221223
766875LV00092B/73/J